Champion's Choice

Also by John R. Tunis

IRON DUKE
THE DUKE DECIDES
THE KID FROM TOMKINSVILLE
WORLD SERIES
ALL-AMERICAN
KEYSTONE KIDS
ROOKIE OF THE YEAR
YEA! WILDCATS!
A CITY FOR LINCOLN

ODYSSEY CLASSIC

Champion's Choice

JOHN R. TUNIS

With an Introduction by Bruce Brooks

An Odyssey Classic
Harcourt Brace Jovanovich, Publishers
San Diego   New York   London

Library of Congress Cataloging-in-Publication Data
Tunis, John Roberts, 1889–
Champion's choice/John R. Tunis;
with an introduction by Bruce Brooks.
p. cm.
"An Odyssey classic."
Summary: Recounts a girl's rise to stardom on the tennis courts,
the conflicts brought by her sport career, and her eventual
retirement in favor of marriage.
ISBN 0-15-216074-4 (pbk.)
[1. Tennis—Fiction.] I. Title.
PZ7.T8236Ch   1990
[Fic]—dc20   89-24485

Printed in the United States of America
A B C D E

CONTENTS

Introduction

John Tunis spent many years as a sports correspondent, traveling across the United States and Europe to cover all manner of events, amateur and professional. Although we tend to regard the 1940s as rather primitive, many things about our contemporary sports scene would not at all surprise Tunis: that professional sports (and the quasi-professional college programs made in their image) have such a major role in the entertainment industry that amateur clubs have become the subject of indifference and even disdain; that males still generally dominate those sports; that the grim severity of pro sports personalities such as Larry Bird or Mike Tyson signifies, for us, a commendable professionalism and competitiveness—"After all," we say, "this is his *work*, not just a game." Young kids who twenty years ago might have been shooting makeshift pucks on frozen rivers are now dressed in uniforms, ordered about by coaches, and getting up at 3:00 A.M. to get ice time on city rinks. And professional athletics are often touted—by adults first, then by kids—as a wonderful ladder out of the ghetto to a life of wealth and glory, which ignores the fact that a person has a mathematically better chance of, say, being elected to the U.S. Congress than of even warming the bench for an NBA team.

Champion's Choice is the novel in which Tunis takes on many of these issues. It is the warm, thrilling, and sometimes frightening tale of a girl named Janet Johnson, who becomes a tennis prodigy, then a champion, and last—by the narrowest of margins, Tunis would have us believe—a full human being. Tunis makes it clear that by no means is her eventual happiness assured by her former achievements; in fact, he shows how easy it is for championship and human growth to be mutually exclusive.

Tunis pulls us into Janet's tennis adventure from the start, exactly as she herself is pulled in. A friend named Rodney sneaks onto a clay court during an adult lawn party and persuades her to hit balls with him. She smacks a good forehand—witnessed by a champion at the party who gives her a racket—and she is hooked. Her father builds her a rebound game on the garage door; she plays some impressive juniors matches, takes lessons, is supported by one expert after another, and eventually gets to some pretty important matches. She loses a few, then begins to win, and, with perfectly paced rushes of experience and confidence, soon stands atop the world of tennis.

People who know Tunis's work will not be surprised to hear that we are completely caught up in Janet's rise, rooting for her all the way. Nobody writes a sports match better than Tunis, and he understands the interior drama and technique of tennis at least as well as he does baseball, football, and track. Janet is a wonderful character, with high standards and great enthusiasms, and, like her, we simply hold nothing back. When she achieves her first championship, we feel like champs ourselves.

But things are not completely fine for Janet from this point on. Sure, the tennis goes well—but with the rather intrusive help of her old friend Rodney, she begins to notice that her values, happiness, and self-satisfaction seem to be lagging behind her game. It's a slight problem, but the implications for an unpleasant single-mindedness are there. Still, she goes on with tennis. What else can she do? She's the champion, and a graceful champion has obligations to fans, family, and business associates.

In subtly drawing us into the conflict between personality and game, between human nature and artificial heroism, Tunis shows that sports matches aren't the only dramas he understands. He is no less adroit with the tactics and shifts in emotional conflicts. Although Janet too readily takes Rodney's critical words to be law, Tunis allows us to be slightly ahead of the champion in seeing that her spontaneity and softness are in peril. She catches and ultimately passes us in wits, though—no one could foresee the ending Janet boldly strikes to her story.

Champion's Choice is another of Tunis's great books in which he shows us that a champion's story is significant not because the protagonist is a celebrity but rather because he or she is a human being. Steinbeck has his workers, Jane Austen her country upper-classes, John le Carré his spies— and Tunis his athletes. In these and many other cases, the writer may appear to be writing about a character's environment and specific tasks but is really holding up for study the importance of the individual *sans* trophies. In this book, the illusions of heroism we have about such people is itself the subject, and the great revelation is that often they have the same illusion about themselves.

It is certain that *Champion's Choice* will draw fire for its seeming sexism. It is true that as Rodney strolls through the book Janet listens avidly to his every word as if it were searing truth. If the champion's boldest choice at the end makes us squirm because it looks so much like a woman tagging along after a strong male, we can be excused; but we should also remember that before her shocking decision, Janet makes an even bigger one in ignoring Rodney's loudest plea. This establishes clearly that her final choice is hers alone, made for herself with her own future at stake. It is not at all difficult to imagine Tunis—who certainly did not share the illusions of male superiority assumed by so many in his time and milieu—writing a story in which a male athlete is turned toward the truth by a woman's critique. In fact, we have only to read *The Duke Decides* to see this happen, more naturally in fact than happens with Janet in this novel.

Janet's choice is not specifically a *woman's* choice; it is a human choice. At Wimbledon in 1989, John McEnroe explained why he was happier as a semifinalist than he had been five years ago as a three-time champion: "I was so caught up in winning the next tournament, and the next, and staying Number One, that the moments I should have been enjoying as a person—the championship moments—passed right by in the tension. Now I have a good marriage and kids, and those are real achievements." Tom Watson said nearly the same thing, after the third round of the 1989 British Open golf tournament, about a title he won five times but had not come close to in five years: "When I was winning, I was thinking only of the next victory, the next challenge to my position at the top. I was too pressed to look around and notice that things should have been enjoyable."

Fifty years ago Tunis wrote the story that McEnroe and Watson are now living. He had a model of his own: a young woman named Florence Farley, who won major tennis championships while still a teenager and who rose to the cold heights of money-mad championship as a substitute for the kind of life Janet Jackson grasps for at the finish of *Champion's Choice*. In fact, a journalistic profile of Farley that Tunis published in *Harper's* in 1929 uses some of the same scenes and quotations we find in the novel. Farley was revered for her "professionalism," and Tunis suffered (rather gladly, it must be said) a fusillade of harsh reactions from a sports world that wished her to remain on her pedestal. His answer was *Champion's Choice*, and whatever Farley's fate, we can now look at someone like McEnroe and believe that Tunis's perceptiveness was not askew.

—Bruce Brooks

1

The Old Center

The sun beat down on the Old Center. It was a warm, mellow sun, the sunshine of spring, hinting of summer and richer, happier days. Aunt Susie at the moment was busily engaged in beating a rug from the open window on the second floor, when through the cadences Janet, who was playing outside, heard the telephone tinkling. She also heard her mother's answering voice. This she was able to do because Aunt Susie had paused and was listening, too.

"Hello . . . who . . . oh, yes . . . yes . . . how do you do?" There was a distinct change in her mother's intonation, and Janet was immediately attracted. She turned up the walk and onto the porch with quick, deft steps, her pigtails flying. Inside the door which she closed gently as she entered, stood her mother at the telephone hanging on the wall.

"Oh . . ." Then there was a long period in which the person at the other end talked interminably. Janet seated herself with interest on a chair, her eyes opening wider and wider. The conversation went on. "Why, yes . . . well, Mr. Johnson couldn't, I'm afraid, Mrs. Davis . . ." Ah, then it was Rodney Davis's mother. Perhaps a birthday party, with ice cream and cake and a magician who did tricks. No, because Rodney had had one only a month before. Her mother continued. "Yes . . . oh, thank you, she's very well, yes, she would love to come. The 25th. Thank you very much. Good-bye."

"Well . . ." She turned to catch the open eyes of Janet and the open mouth of Aunt Susie at the top of the stairs. ". . . a garden party for the District Nurse. On the 25th. Dear me, I hope it won't mean spending more money there, what with the Community Chest, and . . ."

"But, Mother dear, can I go? Can I go, Mother? I want to go awfully."

"Of course, Janet. Now run along and play."

The Garden Party was perfectly organized, with tickets at a dollar and a half apiece, on sale all over town. But tickets were readily disposed of nevertheless. One paid that just to get into the Davis place because the gardens at Marchmont were famous in the spring. Janet, in ecstasy from the moment she awoke on the morning of the 25th, felt that this was indeed a mighty, a stupendous occasion. In the family's aged Buick they rode down the hill, puffed through town, and covered the two miles to the knoll on which stood Marchmont, home of the Davis family. At one side of the winding drive were parked dozens of cars, and Janet, already impressed, felt she had never seen so many cars in one place before. With her observant eye she noticed the license plates of two nearby states, and as they rolled up to the entrance she could hear a band playing. They disembarked and, presenting their tickets to the stern-faced Mr. O'Reilly who usually took tickets in the Gem Movie Palace, entered the grounds.

If Mrs. Davis charged profiteer prices, it must be admitted she gave value. In a tent below the house ice cream and strawberries were being served, as much, so Janet was to discover, as you could eat. The gardens were at their best. Masses of color ranged in terraces brought forth polite exclamations from the crowd moving along the narrow walks, looking at the greenhouses in which were exotic plants Mrs. Davis had collected in various parts of Europe. Janet was excited, and no wonder.

Then Mrs. Davis bore down on them. She was fluttering from one group to another, and pounced on the two visitors from the Hill. She saw before her a tallish woman and a wide-eyed little girl in a big floppy straw hat.

"How do you do, Mrs. Johnson. How good of you to come down. Is this your dear little girl?" Before the other could reply, the dear little girl suddenly uttered a terrific shriek.

"My ribbon . . . my ribbon . . ." Winding his agile way through the sightseers was a small boy who grasped in one hand the big blue bow which had been affixed to Janet's hair with such attention by Aunt Susie.

"Rodney! Rodney . . . come here." The wanderers along the garden paths turned after a little boy who halted reluctantly in full flight. He

4

wore a stiff white collar, a big red necktie, and a stylish blue suit, plainly in honor of the event. He drew near and, extending the bow, said in a low tone and a manner indicating this was not the first time in his life he had apologized,

"I'm-very-sorry-I-pulled-yer-hair-c'mon-lemme-show-yer-the-turtles."

Janet glanced at her mother, seeing assent in her expression. The bow was replaced, retied, and the two moved away. Mrs. Davis expressed the opinion that since Rodney had gone away to school he was a changed boy, that she really did not know how to handle him. Rodney must have heard but gave no evidence of hearing as they moved soberly down the lawn. Among the crowd of chattering strangers and beside this superlatively dressed young man, Janet felt far from home and uncomfortable. When he suggested they stop in the tent for strawberries and ice cream first, she was relieved.

"I've had three already," he whispered. "We'll come back, huh, an' have some more after we've seen the turtles." Accordingly the turtles were visited and inspected in the pond by the rock garden and then again they repaired to the tent, the supplies of strawberries and ice cream apparently as endless as ever. He took her down to a deserted end of the long table and served them both copiously with a large spoon.

"Master Rodney! Master Rodney! Now that's your fifth plate. You get away from this table. I shall have to tell your mother . . ."

A tall figure in a black uniform bore down upon them. The boy hastily dropped the plate without a word and walked away. Janet, taking one long, last spoonful of the delicious stuff, dropped hers, too.

"Aw, he always spoils everything. C'mon down and see the new puppies. No, I tell yer, we'll watch the tennis."

"The what?"

"The exhibition. Exhibition tennis for the District Nurse Fund. Mother has two champions staying here now. You know . . ."

Janet didn't know at all. However, if it was for the District Nurse Fund it must be all right. She vaguely felt she should rejoin her mother, but the crowd carried them along and her mother was nowhere in sight. So she let herself be urged in one direction by the heir of the house of Davis who was pulling her off to the side, until finally they were separated from the throng, under a large pine tree. He grasped one of the lower branches. "Here," he said, and started to climb.

She hesitated only a minute. Up she went, and once safely at his side on a large bough an entrancing spectacle stretched before them. The visitors had spread themselves out all over the sloping lawns which encircled a kind of enclosure. This was surrounded by a high wire netting, and inside the netting were two goddesses in short skirts, hitting a ball. They were all in white, and they moved with easy strides across the enclosure, back and forth, from one side to the other, striking the ball with an air of complete and final authority. Janet, hanging to the branch, watched intently, captured by their sureness and mastery. It accorded with her mood, with the excitement of the fete, with the plates of strawberries and ice cream repeated, with her best white muslin dress stiff and starched for the moment, with her big hat, worn only on important occasions. When one of the goddesses below performed some unbelievably impossible gymnastic the crowd applauded and Janet, sitting uncomfortably on the bough, applauded also. This was indeed living. She missed nothing going on in the enclosure below, until all at once the goddesses stopped.

"Oh . . ." said Janet.

"That's all right," said Rodney with assurance, feeling the disappointment in her voice. "That's all right. After the second set they always stop. They'll be back."

In fact the goddesses, with Mrs. Davis at their side, were trooping to the tent for refreshment. She watched them disappear and observed the air of deference with which they were greeted by the crowd. Then Rodney started to climb down. "C'mon." She did not know what he was doing, but she had confidence that one so full of the ways of the world could make no mistake, and followed obediently to the ground. Rodney wandered over to the chairs at one side where the goddesses had left their implements. Janet fingered one of the instruments, and touched the white fuzzy ball. Then she noticed Rodney.

"Hey!" He nodded in a way that demanded obedience. Standing in the middle of the enclosure, he had one of the implements in his hand

and two balls in the other hand. "Get over there."
He pointed to the other side of the net, brandishing the strange weapon in his hand in a knowledgeable manner.

Her heart jumped, although no one was around.
"Oh, I wouldn't dare. . . . I wouldn't dare. . . ."

"Aw, why not? It's all right. I know Miss Davison, she won't care. Get over there and I'll show yer."

Janet hung her big hat on the post, looked about to be sure no one was watching, and stepped to the other side of the net. He hit a ball across and she rushed at it, swung as she had seen the goddesses do, and . . . missed it completely. Rodney threw back his head and laughed, to her dismay.

"No, no. Now I'm gonna show yer. Keep yer eyes on it, like this." He leaned over earnestly and hit another ball over the net. Then another, and another. To Janet's intense vexation, she swung each time without touching the ball at all. The next time she waited, more cautious, struck it awkwardly, but did return it. "There . . . that's better, see?" He scampered to the side for more balls. "Don't hurry, you hurry too much, just wait . . . now then, once more." Another ball flew at her, and another and another. Clumsily, with some effort, she returned them to him. He continued feeding balls to her while she realized that there was more science to this thing than one would suppose. Suddenly he hit one to the side, far out of her reach.

But the concentrated little girl had not relaxed. With two leaps she had reached the ball. The racquet in her outstretched arm caught it cleanly and sent it low, swift, and sure across the net. It whizzed past the little boy who was totally unprepared for such perfection. His face expressed annoyance as the ball shot by; after all it is disturbing for a pupil thus to show up the master. Before he could speak a quiet voice broke in.

"Splendid."

Janet looked up. One of the goddesses was standing beside the net, smiling as she wiped her face with a towel. "Come here," she said, encouragingly. Janet obeyed quickly, reflecting that she had not seen her mother for some time, that her white dress was rumpled and torn, covered with pitch and ruined from sitting on the branch of the tree. As she put on her hat she felt her partner in crime making himself inconspicuous, for already observers were straggling back to the court. The goddess knelt down, beckoned, and while Janet braced herself for what was to come she observed that the face before her was kind, with wrinkles about the corners of the eyes.

"How long have you been playing, my dear?" Janet's lower lip quivered, but she kept a difficult control of herself. "Only . . . about . . . five minutes." At this remark the goddess for some unaccountable reason threw back her head and laughed. The culprit was reassured but not wholly reassured.

"No . . . I mean how many times have you played? . . . Is this your first time?" The floppy hat flapped violently up and down. The goddess leaned way over so she could look into her face, and said slowly, "The first time . . . you ever hit this . . . this ball?" Again the hat flopped.

"Janet! Oh, dear, I do hope she hasn't ruined your racquet. I'd simply no idea where the child was. Your dress . . . Janet . . . What have you . . ." Janet knew instantly by the tone and the implications in that voice she had done wrong. But the goddess merely rose and smiled.

"Oh, not at all. She hasn't hurt it a bit. I was interested because I watched her playing and saw her hit the ball just now. She has an unusually natural style. Has she ever taken lessons?" Now Mrs. Johnson was mystified.

"Why, no. I don't believe she ever saw a tennis racquet before." The goddess leaned down again over Janet who by this time had taken refuge close to her parent's skirt.

"Never seen a racquet before? Really? Well, then I'm going to make you a present of this racquet here. Some day she'll be a good little player. Now, my dear," and she handed Janet the racquet, "now just go out there and show us all how you hit the ball the way you did when I came along."

Janet grasped the racquet firmly by the handle and mumbled her confused thanks. She looked round at the growing circle of interested listeners, at Mrs. Davis who was not a comforting sight as she towered in the rear, at the other goddess standing by one side, at the empty enclosure beside which the crowd was gathering. Then she shook her head, slowly but with finality. It was plain from her manner that Janet had a mind of her own. To be sure, she said nothing, but solemnly continued to shake her head.

For she knew when to let well enough alone; a knowledge more priceless than a college education.

2

One New Tennis Ball

Late summer. A generous September sun beat over the hillside, cast a drowsy spell over the houses and inhabitants and the animals like Mr. Brown's airedale which lay stretched in the middle of the road exactly as if he had been run over. The atmosphere was heavy and the distant mountains were shut off from view. Janet, though she belonged to this life, was for the moment of it but not in it. Through the open window came the click-click, click-click of Alvah Stone's mowing machine as it moved relentlessly through the rowen, the cries of four barefooted boys playing several houses away, and the exultant barking of the Raymonds' little terrier which was a signal that the Raymond children were going berrying on the slopes of the Hill. Still she remained inside, at work. It was lesson time.

The doctor had advised that Janet be kept out of doors until she got older and stronger. This, however, for the practical-minded Mrs. Johnson, did not mean she should run loose all day. She went ahead in a determined manner to plan systematically for the education of her daughter. Janet must work, study, and play with the sun. Thus in winter it was arranged she was to be outdoors during the warmest parts of the day between ten and three. Her studying was before and after these hours. In summer when the days were long, her working periods came in the afternoon when it was too hot to play out-of-doors.

Secretly Janet was rather ashamed of this arrangement. It disturbed her that she was always working when other children were playing, and playing when they were working. It was certainly difficult to place one's attention on geography when the windows were open and sounds and noises kept drifting in, such fascinating evidences of life in process around. She reflected that things were invariably more interesting outside whenever she started to study. Her reflections were so deep that it was necessary for her mother to remind her this was study hour.

"Three times I asked you, dear." Dimly she realized that Janet was growing older, and that in the process she was getting more "difficult." If only she would stay this age forever. . . .

"Connecticut? Come now, Janet."

"Hartford?"

"Rhode Island?" Ah, Rhode Island. This was always a disturbing point in Janet's life.

"Oh, dear, I never can remember R'd Island."

"But think. You got it day before yesterday."

Click-click, click-click—click-click, went that diverting machine below. Summoning her utmost powers of concentration Janet was unable to remember Rhode Island.

"Very well." Mrs. Johnson wrote the word Providence on a large sheet of paper. This meant Janet had to copy it twenty times afterward.

"Pennsylvania?"

"Pittsburgh!"

"No."

"I mean Harrisburg."

"That's better. Maine?"

"Augusta."

"Very good. That will do for geography. To-morrow you have three states to learn, and I do hope you won't forget Rhode Island again. Now your composition."

Janet liked writing; writing was no task to her. Every other day she wrote with much pleasure a short composition on some one subject of her choice. The next day her mother corrected it by reading it aloud at her side exactly as it had been written, while Janet stood watching, the better to observe the mistakes she had committed. Just as she rose to go around the table to the end where her mother was seated, a long and unmelodious whistle penetrated the room. Janet jumped. Silence, then the whistle was repeated.

"Oh, Mother! That's Rodney Davis! Now . . . he's come up to play tennis with me."

Mrs. Johnson was less disturbed by the whistle than her daughter. "Very well, Janet, he must wait, that's all." Once more the whistle sounded, sharper, more unmusical than ever. The composition in her hand, Mrs. Johnson left the dining room and went to the front door. Sitting on his bicycle, one foot on the stone carriage block before the house, was a tanned boy quite evidently outgrowing the machine. He was casting a contemplative gaze over the house. Lashed to his handlebars was a racquet; she wondered how his legs could move with this handicap, for he was now bigger than the boy of the garden party of four months before.

"I'm sorry, Rodney. Janet is studying. She won't be able to come out for half an hour."

The boy looked at her and took off his cap with a mechanical gesture. "Yes'm," he said, starting to dismount.

"You may wait if you wish, Rodney."

"Yes'm." Quite plainly he intended to do so. He was placing his bicycle against the stone block, while the four bare-legged berry pickers viewed the proceedings with interest from a distance. Mrs. Johnson returned to the dining room and an inattentive pupil. The mind of the girl was fastened upon that game with the visitor; nothing, it appeared, could bring it back. So short was their period of daily work, so obedient was Janet as a rule, that discipline was something rarely known in the educational program of the family. For once, however, the teacher ventured to suggest punishment.

"But, Mother . . . he may be gone. He may not wait." A half hour was endless. It was eternal.

"That makes no difference, dear. This is your study time." The teacher was firm, while Janet deplored, as she so often had before, the fate that forced her to work while others played.

"Come back, now." Janet was at the bay window of the dining room trying to see whether the bicycle was against the carriage block in front. It was. Mrs. Johnson began reading the girl's writing effort as her daughter reluctantly shuffled to her side.

The task seemed endless. Mrs. Johnson knew it would consume just about the twenty minutes left of the lesson period. Janet sat down with a deep sigh against the injustices of life. Whether the agony was worse, whether the twenty minutes seemed more endless for the girl or her parent is debatable. It is also questionable who was the happier when the first chime from the parlor announced the advent of three o'clock.

With a whoop of joy she flew from the room, burst through the front door and onto the lawn. Mrs. Johnson, putting away the books and papers that covered the dining room table, watched them pass before the window, and heard Rodney say as he held out a brand-new white ball:

"My dad gave it to me. It's brand-new." Janet took it and fingered it tenderly. Her balls, Mrs. Johnson reflected, were old, gray, worn smooth. She went back into the kitchen and from the window watched them playing in the sunken garden which Will Johnson in his rare moments of leisure had fashioned into a kind of court. Rodney, she noticed, was growing fast. Then when the two stood near each other by the net she realized Janet was also growing. Living with her one didn't appreciate it. Though Rodney was almost two years older, he was little taller than Janet. Better still, her legs were sturdier, her arms firmer than they had been. Standing at the window watching she also noticed that the child was improving at the game, that she was hitting more balls over the net and into the opposing court, and fewer into Mr. Brown's grapevine adjoining the garden.

Half an hour or more later she was in an

upstairs bedroom that gave on the garden, when she heard a squeal of delight.

"Six to four. That's two sets to me, Rodney."

His voice was less jubilant. "Yeh." There was a pause. "You better give me back my ball now. I hafta go home."

3

Joining the Country Club

Janet was thirteen when the family moved from Millville to Greenwood Heights, a suburb of New York some thirty miles out of town. There were advantages and disadvantages in their new home. One of the latter was the lack of space for her to play which she had in the Old Center at Millville.

Mrs. Johnson saw this immediately and suggested it to her husband. "Will Johnson, you must do something about it." Whenever she called him "Will Johnson" he knew she meant business. Standing before the fireplace he looked at her in his quiet way.

"H'm," he replied. As if to say, "I am giving it my earnest consideration." But she was not satisfied with his earnest consideration.

"But here 'tis June, and that child has no place to play in. She hasn't anyone to play with except those little Putnam girls who are younger than she is."

He turned and knocked his pipe against the fireplace. "Any public tennis courts in town?" He observed a shadow over his wife's forehead. "I suppose you looked that up," he added hastily. "Then this Country Club they talk about—"

"You know as well as I do that's impossible. We can't afford it."

Early the next morning Will Johnson was up and about to see, as he expressed it to himself, what could be done. He wore a pair of old trousers and a faded yellow flannel shirt, open at the neck, as he stepped out on the back porch with a spirit level and a steel tape in his chubby fingers.

When he stumbled upstairs to bed the previous evening he had vaguely intended to make some kind of a practice board against which Janet could knock her precious tennis ball, and obtain some exercise combined with a little fun. He had thought of a board ten or twelve feet high against which she could bat the ball; this would amuse her, it would give her the exercise she needed. But as he stood on the back porch whistling softly between his teeth, he soon saw that the question wasn't as easy to solve as all that.

On one side of their rented property which did not extend much beyond the confines of the dwelling, was a board fence, while on the other side was a high wire fence. Unfortunately, also, the tiny space of the Johnson domain was cut up by various things: a cement path came round the side of the house and led up to the back door, and almost in the middle of the small back-yard was a stout, rounded pole. From the top of this pole to four other stout, rounded poles set in the corners of the enclosure was a clothesline. Even if the center pole were taken down, he saw that enough room was lacking to make the small-est kind of a tennis court. Yes, the problem was more complex than it appeared.

Sitting down on the top step of the back porch, he lit his pipe. On both sides extended a row of yards, similar to his own. The front lawn was diminutive. He thought vaguely of renting a patch of land and building Janet a practice board, but this had obvious drawbacks. It was hardly likely he could find land anywhere near the house. The more he thought, the harder the problem became. Yet it was really a simple matter. It was only necessary to make the garage door a practice board. And there you were!

He placed the spirit level carefully down on the top step and walked hastily round the house, fearing lest something should spoil the delightful simplicity of his idea. The dwelling had been built for one family; but the contractor had a two-car mind. From the street a wide cement roadway, twenty feet across, led to the door of the garage. The idea of the builder, however, had been more fertile than his capital; he was therefore obliged to construct a one-car garage in order to cut his costs somewhat. So the road narrowed when it drew near the entrance like a kind of inverted Y. On the outside the door of the garage was smooth. The wide driveway of cement was an ideal surface. Here was the perfect practice board for Janet already made!

It was not yet breakfast time, but Janet was

already awake. She must have felt something in the air because when called she came armed with her racquet and a ball; a ball from which the cover had been divorced by months of constant use. At his order she stood outside on the cement walk and hit balls against the smooth surface of the door, while he stayed inside watching their effect upon the framework, seeing whether bracing in certain points might not be necessary.

Bang! "All right, lower down."

Bang! "That's it, now to the left."

Bang! "Higher."

Bang! "No, still higher."

Bang! "Fine. Now wait a minute until I just mark that place. Now, once more."

Bang-bang!

The barrage which was lifted shortly before breakfast was resumed shortly after dinner that afternoon. For an hour Janet pushed balls diligently against the door without, while her father within noted their effect. Will Johnson liked to work with his hands; the supports to strengthen the door from the battering it was to receive were cleverly and competently made. They held firm so there was no undue strain upon them. His task finished, he came outside carrying a pot of white paint, a brush, and a long flat ruler.

"What's all that for, Father?"

"You'll see." Standing on a low, wooden box he began to measure the door. A wise father, he knew his child; knew also that merely hitting a ball against that blank wall would become boring sooner or later. Somehow he must devise a game; something for her to play against. This he proceeded to do.

Like the house, the garage and the door were a dark greenish color. With careful hands he painted a white square border in the center of the door. A larger square, and then a third larger than the second, and a fourth larger than the third. In the smallest square he marked a large 10. In the second square he put a 9, then an 8 and so on almost to the edge of the door.

"Now, Janet, see, this is how you play the game. Give me your racquet a minute."

"No, no, Father, I know, I know. I understand, I wanna try myself." She hit the ball against the door. "Four, two . . . three . . . eight—oh, eight, Daddy, eight, I did an eight . . . two . . . one. . . ."

"Yes . . . well . . . let me have it just a second." He reached for her, but he might as well have attempted to catch the moon. Darting back and forth, behind him, in front, now to one side, now to the other, she was hitting the ball against the door with considerable skill. Her training in the old sunken garden at Millville had not been wasted. He watched her, amused, interested in her tense eagerness.

"That white paint isn't completely dry yet, Janet, and it's going to spoil your ball and your racquet." Actually it was doing that; the ball was daubed with splotches of white which had in turn communicated themselves to the racquet until it resembled a checkerboard. But Janet, concentrated, went on.

"Two . . . one . . . four . . . oh, dear, I missed it." Her father shook his head and went inside to wash after his labors. An hour later he chanced to look out of the side window.

"Milly. Oh, Milly, come here a minute. You upstairs? Just look out that bedroom window."

Mrs. Johnson walked over and looked down on an amazing scene. Mr. Putnam next door was standing beside the fence, apparently waiting for an invitation to come over and play himself. In the meantime he was attempting to coach one of his daughters who was rarely even hitting the door. At the end of the driveway were most of the children in the neighborhood, certainly the entire juvenile population of Walnut Street, opened-eyed and open-mouthed. They were straggling in some sort of a line, hoping for a turn at this new and fascinating sport. Some had old-fashioned racquets, some had new balls, and Mrs. Johnson noticed that the ball in use was not Janet's old gray one, but new, white, and clean.

"That's all of your turn, Alice." Her child was talking in an authoritative tone. "You had your ten tries." Janet was the marshal of the forces, the generalissimo of the game; not only because it belonged to her but by right of conquest. "No! You can't play any more." With a jump she was across the drive and had snatched the racquet from the hand of the little girl.

"Janet!" She looked up to see her mother at the window. "You must not snatch things. Ask Alice for it politely, like a lady."

Her daughter looked annoyed. "I ast her." She enunciated slowly and distinctly. "I ast her, I ast her, and I ast her. They won't stop when they get playing. They wanna keep on all afternoon." She turned to her cohorts in the rear who were silently waiting the royal dispensation.

"Now I'm fourteen. Buddy Rogers, he made eight. And Junior had seven. Whose turn next? Your turn?" A tiny lad at the head of the indefinite line nodded eagerly. "All right, d'ja bring your own ball?" In the dining room window Mr. Johnson turned away with a smile on his face. He foresaw occupation in the open air for his active-minded and active-limbed daughter for some time to come.

Some children might have tired of the game, might have found it monotonous. Not Janet. She was always trying to improve her best score, to hit any square any time from any position on the drive. Because of this persistence her skill increased rapidly. Quick, nimble, agile, she was always in a spot to strike the ball, she soon knew the exact place it would bounce, depending on the severity with which it was hit. Gradually she became able to make the most amazing recoveries, to put the ball into the center square time and time again. When she was alone, which was not often because the fame of the sport had spread over the juvenile population of Greenwood Heights like an attack of measles, she would attempt to hit the square a certain number of times in succession. Once outside that inner square she started all over. In the warm summer evenings her father would sit beside the drive on the grass, smoking his after dinner pipe and counting.

"Twenty-one, twenty-two, twenty-three, twenty-four, twenty-five, twenty-six. . . . OUT."

"Oh, Father! Well, that's only the second time I've ever done twenty-five." Then at the request of one or two newcomers who stood waiting for a chance to take part, she would announce:

"No, I can't play with you. I'm playing with my daddy this evening." This did not dissuade the hangers-on, however, for they immediately took seats on the grass and remained to applaud her feats.

Seeing her play, Will Johnson feared the game might become too easy were there no more worlds for Janet to conquer. So he painted two more small squares, one on each corner of the door near the top. So difficult were these to hit that only Janet attempted them; they were not for the ordinary player. Nevertheless, the game maintained and increased its hold on the youthful population of the Heights. This was due to several causes. First, it was a novelty, and moreover a novelty not too difficult to learn in its first steps. Second, its champion was originator of the sport. Respect for Janet grew, and the Johnson driveway was lined with boys and girls waiting their turn at this fascinating game. Other garage doors were fitted up, other cement walks brought into use; none supplanted the first in popularity. The place became Janet's Country Club. In fact directly the 6:19 pulled in at the station each evening, there would be a squawking of horns at the end of the blind street upon which the Johnsons lived, as the sedans of the neighborhood called the youth of the Heights to supper and bed.

Meanwhile by right of conquest in battle, Janet reigned supreme. Older girls and older boys from time to time were imported to contest her superiority; invariably they retired beaten in short order. Janet acted as arbiter and mistress of her kingdom; she made the rules, saw they were obeyed, settled disputes; this ball touched the line, that one did not, the next was on the cement; she was the person appealed to. Gradually she played less and less with children. If she took up a challenge she took it merely to dispose of some pretender to the throne. The thing she cared most about was hitting the ball alone into the corners with her father sitting cross-legged on the grass, counting and pulling his pipe in approval. There only was the challenge to her eye, the spur to her brain and muscle.

4

Test of Character

All fall, and indeed all winter whenever the ground was free of snow, Janet was to be found playing against her door. So sure, so precise, so accurate did she become that she could perform the most unbelievable feats with the ball. Thus she would hit the square, any square you named, any number of times in succession. Nor did her ardor diminish as her skill increased. She was never satiated with the game, never bored with playing, always eager to attempt a new record, continually breaking existing ones and moving on to planes of greater sureness. If anyone in the family felt the inability to join the Country Club on account of the expense, it was certainly not the youngest member.

Then quite unexpectedly the next spring they joined. It appeared that every member of the Club was permitted as many junior memberships as he liked for his children at fifteen dollars a year. Janet was to be given a junior membership although her parents officially were not members and equally officially not recognized by the authorities in charge. She paid no initiation fee and nothing but the children's membership. All this developed through the father of Jimmy Clements, one of the youngsters she was forever beating at her door game. His father had strolled over one day and watched Janet devouring her prey on the cement walk. Several weeks later he spoke to Will Johnson on the eight-two train in the morning. Explaining the situation at the Club, he invited Janet to become a junior member.

The orthodox game played on the open court at the Club was, so Janet found, little different from the unorthodox game against the garage door. Save that it was easier. The door never made mistakes. You could not fool the door. The door never missed. Against the door, the ball always came back. Whereas human beings, even older and wiser human beings, did make mistakes. They did miss, they did make errors. It was all so absurdly simple, so delightful after that relentless door, it was magnificent fun, it was exhilarating. Boys and girls, young and old, as well as the majority of grown-up players at the Club fell before her confident racquet just as the children upon Walnut Street had done on the cement driveway. Inside of four months "that little Johnson girl" was known to all the younger and many of the older members.

Janet was now thirteen, growing rapidly, intensely interested in life, excessively busy. There was the school she now attended which was her cross; then her lessons at home which she found hard to master. Never having attended school, those first years were a trial. Then there were her singing lessons. It happened there was an especially fine singing teacher in the Heights, who taught a few specially selected pupils. Mrs.

Burton suggested to Mrs. Johnson that an exchange might be effected. Janet was to give tennis lessons to the Burton youngsters, and Mrs. Burton was to give Janet two singing lessons a week. The idea worked as these ideas seldom do. Janet was the perfect instructor: kind, ingenious in teaching her pupils what she knew, while she soon made the discovery others have before that teaching benefited her own game enormously. Instructing and explaining, she began to ask herself questions, to wonder why she did things a certain way, why, for instance, it was easier to hit a ball when it was not close to her body.

Finally the fame of the little girl began to spread to nearby towns. She was beating the juvenile population of the Heights so easily that Mr. Clements, by no means distressed to find his protégée acquiring a reputation, suggested that Mrs. Richardson who lived in nearby Jamestown should come over and play Janet a couple of sets. Mrs. Richardson, who had at one time been in the First Ten and a player of national reputation, agreed that her opinion on the girl's potentialities might not be without value. Consequently the meeting was arranged for the next

Saturday afternoon. Promptly at three the old, red Buick toiled up the slope to the clubhouse bearing the entire family.

Janet wore a pale blue sailor suit with a square collar which flapped when she ran, a white satin necktie tied in a bow in front, and a skirt flaring at the bottom; the whole having a homespun effect which was natural enough, as it had been designed and constructed by Mrs. Johnson. But she was a fresh and enchanting figure when she stepped down the lawn to the courts beside the older, chattering lady. A queer person indeed, thought Janet. Approaching the court she fired question after question at the little girl. How long had she played? And what kind of racquet did she use? What were her best shots? It is hard to make anyone nervous who does not know what nerves are; but Janet became uneasy as she realized that she hadn't the faintest idea of the answers to most of these questions. She hardly knew one stroke from another, and her racquet had long since lost its trademark through wear and tear.

About the court were several hundred members seated, a fact which also disturbed her somewhat as she stepped into the arena. Then, with the impact of the ball on her racquet, she felt once more the sensation she felt on the cement walk at home. She was master of herself and of that familiar ball. Immediately she forgot the crowd, forgot the stylish lady across the net, and proceeded to place her shots just where she intended they should go. Her accuracy was disconcerting.

All the while, her father and mother remained on the veranda above, seeing yet unseen. There they sat, silent figures noticed by no one, until their child came up the steps toward them, her face red but her bearing triumphant, her pigtails damp with perspiration but her air that of a conqueror. Behind her panted Mrs. Richardson. She had come for a little exercise at the end of which she had expected to dispense some condescending advice. Instead she had been run up and down, from side to side of that court, chasing shots she could never quite get to, reaching for balls that were always too fast and much too accurately placed. She was astonished and upset. She was amazed at the little girl's game. She was breathless.

"Give . . . that child of yours . . . time, Mrs. Johnson . . . give her time . . . and some day . . . she'll be a great player . . ."

5

Junior Championships

The two celebrities sat on the edge of two uncomfortable chairs in the Johnsons' front room: Mr. Simmons, president of the Country Club, and the indefatigable Mr. Clements. Janet stood open-eyed beside her father's rocker, feeling she was the object of their visit, yet wondering what it could portend. Not however until Mrs. Johnson appeared did Mr. Clements get into his subject.

"Now we were thinking, that is to say, a number of us up at the Club were discussing the matter the other day. 'Course nothing definite decided, you understand, but we were just thinking, Will, of sending Janet down to Cold Springs for the Junior Championships next summer."

"Oooh . . ." interjected Janet. "Oooh . . . , Mother, wouldn't that be dandy?" To her, Cold Springs was as inaccessible as Russia. Or Fairyland. But she stopped short as she observed distress on her mother's countenance.

"I'm sorry, Mr. Clements, but who would go with her? The trip would be wonderful and I'd love for her to go, but I couldn't think of letting her . . ."

"Certainly not, Mrs. Johnson. We planned that you should both go."

Mrs. Johnson was startled. "Why, Mr. Clements! Both of us? It would last a whole week. That would cost . . . why . . . a hundred dollars."

"Well . . . yes, p'r'aps it would. But you see it's this way, Mrs. Johnson. There's a number of us at the Club who've been watching your little girl for some time. We've all of us noticed the progress she's made, and we're anxious to give her all the help we possibly can. Now Mr.

Rogers has been talking it over with me; he's influential in the Chamber of Commerce, you know. They think it would be mighty good for the Club and for the town if Janet went down, and he thinks that we, that is they, could find ways of getting you and the young lady to Cold Springs without any expense to you or Mr. Johnson.

"It would be a first-rate vacation, too. Not but what I'm sure our little girl here wouldn't cover herself with glory." The little girl wasn't quite as sure as Mr. Clements. But a trip to Cold Springs . . .

Six months later Duncan Fletcher stood behind the wire netting surrounding one of the courts at Cold Springs. This young man was the vice-president of the Atlantic States Tennis Association and he had charge of the Cold Springs tournament. For a moment he watched the two girls playing, and then with an efficient air walked briskly to another court.

Standing beside the court he was appraising the different entrants, none very promising. Then in the distance he observed a girl in a white sailor suit with a peculiar stroke, a stroke certainly not classical but one that seemed to be effective. She was a sprite upon the court, dancing here, there, never failing to reach the ball, apparently submerging her opponent.

"Who's that on court eight?" he asked a passing official.

"Don't know. She isn't much good, her backhand is weak. I was watching her just now."

He noticed then, as he had not noticed before, that this was true. Janet, playing against the garage door, had always had a tendency to run round a ball on her left side and take it with her forehand. But to compensate for this defect she certainly made few mistakes. He wandered over and watched carefully for ten minutes. Then he returned to the clubhouse, made some inquiries of the referee, and after a conference with the clerk in the hotel he was not surprised to see Janet's name posted on the draw in the first round with the figures, 6–2, 6–2, underneath.

Mrs. Johnson, however, was much surprised to have a nice-looking young man address her in the lobby. It was the more astonishing since no one save bellboys and waiters had spoken to them since their arrival. They had spoken to no one, being a bit dismayed, dazzled by the vast hotel and the dozens of young players with their mothers.

Ten minutes' conversation with Duncan

Fletcher convinced Mrs. Johnson that here was a friend in need. She explained that they had arrived in a downpour and Janet had caught a cold. Their reservations, wired by Mr. Clements, had been distorted into the name of Thompson, and no room was ready for them. All players were to be accommodated, not in the hotel itself, but in the Annex. There was no heat in the Annex. Their room was right over the kitchen. Sleep was impossible after 5:30 A.M. Janet's cold was worse and Mrs. Johnson was seriously considering returning home that night. In fact she had a timetable in her hand.

Right there Janet Johnson's career hung in the balance. Nor is it too much to say that Duncan Fletcher by his quick thinking and quicker action saved her for tennis at this moment. He begged Mrs. Johnson to sit down ten minutes while he went to see what could be done. Only five minutes were necessary. In that time he had routed the referee from dinner and brought him rushing into the lobby full of apologies to Mrs. Johnson for his regrettable lack of attention. A few crisp words from Mr. Fletcher to the clerk had exchanged their room in the Annex for a comfortable one on the fourth floor of the hotel.

Twenty minutes later their baggage was moved, and he visited them upstairs with aspirin for Janet.

Janet went from success to success in the next six days. By Saturday morning she found herself, to her surprise but not Mr. Fletcher's, in the finals against the brilliant young Californian star, Rosalind Kennedy.

It was that afternoon when for the first time Janet realized how much, much more there was to tennis than hitting a ball across a net. Not given to nerves, the preliminaries to the match were sufficient to make even the most stolid a trifle queasy. There were the two cups, the large silver vase for the winner and the tiny one for the runner-up, on a table beside the court. There was the umpire in a special white blazer with a kind of colored design over his pocket. There were linesmen on every line, and ballboys in the rear. Even Mr. Fletcher had a different manner. He was strangely tense and preoccupied as he attended to the last important details; marshaled the photographers who had come for the finals, saw that the balls were ready, stationed the ballboys, measured the net at the center and did a dozen odd jobs. Janet imagined to herself as she watched that the match could hardly have caused more trouble had it been for the senior championships of the United States.

At fourteen, Janet was large for her age, but the Californian, almost two years older, towered above her. The arrangements for the finals had slightly staggered Janet's composure, yet her opponent was strangely unmoved. The two presented a picture at the net, a prey for the photographers before starting play. It was the first time Janet had ever been photographed; she was not sure she liked it, nor the brusque commands of the kneeling men with cameras. She stood in her homemade middy blouse and skirt, her pigtails down her back, a contrast to the older, self-possessed girl, whose hair had been specially waved for the event and who was dashing and smart in a pair of shorts. Will Johnson had managed to buy Janet a new racquet, but her adversary had an armful. Truly an imposing figure.

The photographers finally were satisfied. The two girls went onto the court, rallied, hitting balls across the net for a few minutes while the cameramen clicked anew from the sidelines. Then the match began. Those first finals Janet never forgot. Nor yet the competent player facing her. Rosalind had received good coaching, Californian coaching; she was mature and experienced in competition. Used to playing good boy players, she was able to face anyone and give as good as she got. Both that assured young lady and her strokes were a revelation to Janet.

At the beginning, the clocklike precision of the younger girl prevailed. Rosalind hit hard, hit well, scored points outright despite Janet's remarkable agility, but dropped the first two games. She was tennis-wise, knowing it is better to hit out at first, to drive a few shots over the baseline, if by so doing one can get the range of the court. She soon proceeded to get the range. Her ground strokes gradually became better, she lowered the trajectory and they fell into court. Her service, a beautiful twisting shot which bounced high to Janet's backhand, was a puzzle. Worst of all was her volleying.

To Janet the net was *terra incognita*. She had learned her game against a wall, a sort of baseline game, and even at the Country Club had had no difficulty beating the few boys she played whenever they took the net. But this Californian was different. She not only came to the net, once there she seemed to attract every shot onto her racquet. Her crisp, decisive volleys usually fell out of reach. Overhead she was deadly, smashing to the corners like a boy and seldom missing. Soon games were two-all, two-three, two-four. Janet, red, flushed, now in distress, worried under the barrage of deep drives bombarding her court, made a desperate effort to take the eighth game on her own service but lost it as the Californian finished with a stop volley.

There were things which Janet always remembered. One was a persistent photographer back of the court trying to snap the champion-to-be; his indifference when she was in range and his concentration when Rosalind was on that side. Janet had never seen ballboys before, did not know they existed. Specially hired for the finals, they were clumsy and bothered her by throwing balls carelessly or by tossing them at her when she started to serve. Meanwhile the score mounted in the second set as the blonde Californian, now supremely confident, perceived a weakness in Janet's left side and, attacking her backhand with a deep forcing shot, invariably finished off the point with a sharp volley to the opposite corner. It was terrible. It was humiliating. Janet couldn't bear to look at her mother on the side. Tears came. She tried harder and harder, she pressed, she hadn't the faintest idea what pressing was, but she pressed, she snatched at the ball, hitting too soon, making errors off the easiest of shots.

"Game . . . set . . . and match . . . Miss Kennedy, 6–2, 6–2." The umpire climbed down from his chair as the winner went to pick up her mauve sweater and her six racquets beside his stand. Janet still had her only racquet in her arms. A crowd, or what seemed like a crowd, rushed round the pretty girl in shorts who shook her blonde mane back off her forehead and smiled at the photographers when Duncan Fletcher came up with the Cup. In a minute the ceremony was finished. Still they surrounded the champion. Someone was holding her silver vase. Someone else had her six racquets. Nobody had time for the loser. Janet and her mother turned and started climbing the slopes to the hotel, entirely alone.

6

Progress

It was plain enough that if Janet had great natural tennis ability she had little else. Her strokes were effective if rudimentary, she got the ball over the net, but that was all. She won matches thanks to her sureness and her amazing quickness about the court. But more was necessary. Duncan Fletcher had advised some professional coaching, and explained that there was a Tennis Clinic for youngsters at Jamestown, a large town six miles from the Heights. Moreover, he assured Mrs. Johnson that he could arrange to have Janet enrolled free of charge. What was a Tennis Clinic? A Tennis Clinic, it appeared, was the Tennis Association name for a coaching school. A professional was ready three times a week to give free instruction in strokes and tactics all summer to young players who were recommended.

So three times a week the rest of the summer they drove over to the Country Club at Jamestown for a tennis lesson at the Clinic. Janet was more faithful in attendance than most of the girls in the neighborhood, and with the help of Chalmers, the professional who saw her possibilities, she developed rapidly. By the end of the summer, he suggested that since she was further along than the others, she might come over the next spring for private lessons in which he could concentrate entirely upon her.

Mrs. Johnson was intelligent enough to realize that Janet was immature in many ways, that from every angle it would be better if she stayed out of competition the next summer. This she decided against the wishes of Janet herself who, with the bitter sting of her defeat partly erased by the passage of time, had been looking forward all winter to another exciting excursion to Cold Springs. Mrs. Johnson also made this decision against the wishes of Chalmers, the professional, who considered he had discovered Janet, as well as of Duncan Fletcher who felt precisely the same thing.

Meanwhile Janet practiced hard and relentlessly at Jamestown. She was faithful, she was regular, she was consistent. It was drudgery, not fun. Balls across court from one corner to the other. Balls from the other corner across court. Balls down the line, backhand, forehand. Service. "Throw the ball carefully, Miss Johnson. Like this, see, gently. No; don't joggle. Moment you joggle you lose balance. Balance is jess's important in serving as driving. You couldn't hit your forehand if your body was all a-jiggle, could you? Of course not. Keep your balance, remember how important balance is in tennis. There . . . that's better. Now try it again. And again . . . here's a ball, try it again . . . there." And so on and so on, day after day in one of the hottest summers Jamestown ever knew.

Many more youngsters are spoiled by being pushed at an early age than by any other cause. Janet developed slowly, but she developed. She was no longer a master of the garage-door game only; she was master of the court as well. Yet in wet weather and during the colder months she kept her hand and eye in practice against her favorite door. Meanwhile her diet, her sleep, her movements, her whole life gradually became dominated by the desire to atone for the defeat at Cold Springs. The next summer when she was sixteen, she and her mother returned again. Rosalind Kennedy had graduated from the junior ranks; there were three other Californians, but they were not as good as Rosalind and moreover Janet was equal to them now. Without the loss of a single set she achieved her ambition and became Junior Champion.

"What a difference!" thought her mother, watching Janet escorted by Duncan Fletcher and surrounded by congratulating admirers after the match. In the big lobby of the hotel stood a long table covered with food and drink, behind it were servitors in uniform. Mrs. Johnson, exhausted by the events of the afternoon, sank into a chair. Indeed the match had taken far more out of her than out of her daughter. Janet, excited, flushed, exultant, happy, approached the table.

"How wonderfully you played. . . . Here, do

have some ginger ale . . . a Coke? You were simply marvelous . . . simply . . ." Congratulations on every side. Ah, victory was sweet. They pressed drinks and food upon her.

"Thank you. Oh, thank you. Thanks, Mr. Fletcher. Thanks so much. Yes, I'll have a Coke, please. And some lemonade for Mother, please." She glanced round to see her weary mother sitting in a far corner.

"A Coke? Yes, indeed. Won't you have some of this cake, too?" Mr. Fletcher was offering her the cake. Janet regarded it with attention. It was a large, round layer cake, a very masterpiece of a cake with thick, rich frosting. The happy look faded from her eyes. Her mouth suddenly shut tight, her head went over on one side as though she were surveying the cake from every possible angle. There it dangled temptingly before her nose. And eyes.

"Well . . .", she said, after a longish pause. "Well," and she looked quickly at Duncan Fletcher. "You see, I'm not allowed to eat cake. It's bad for the wind. I'm in training, you see. But mayn't I just take this piece over to Mother so I can touch it and smell it?"

7

Ordeal by Battle

Janet was trying hard to sleep in the hot twilight of an August night in the Forest Hills Inn. With the applause from that last terrific forehand drive which had beaten Rosalind Kennedy still echoing, with the praise and congratulations still ringing in her ears, life seemed sweet. Was she then, really, the second youngest player ever to reach the finals of the Championships? Think of it! Twelve months before she had been an unknown girl from Greenwood

Heights winning the junior singles at Cold Springs. Now, a finalist against Irene Gordon, she had reached the last round in her first national championships.

She was frightfully tired yet sleep was impossible. Her head hummed, buzzed, throbbed with excitement. Eleven struck from the tower chimes. She might win tomorrow, she must win tomorrow, she would win tomorrow . . . her brain whirled like a dynamo. The longer she lay there exhausted and sleepless, the more nervous she became. Tonight of all nights, when she needed rest so badly, why, oh, why could she get no sleep? She tried hard to sleep, but sleep eluded her. So the minutes passed and another hour tolled from the wretched chimes. Without any warning she burst into tears.

She did not have any intention of crying, in fact she hardly knew why she was crying. Yet she couldn't stop. Somehow it was a relief. Softly, in order not to wake her parents in the next room, she sobbed into her pillow. How long this went on she had no idea. The next thing she knew her mother was moving round the bed and the summer sunshine was seeping in through the drawn curtains at the windows.

Yes, she had slept. She had slept more than she realized because it was after ten o'clock. Already? Her mother informed her that in an hour lunch would appear, that it was both breakfast and lunch combined. She rose, washed, and rather against her mother's wishes glanced at the sports pages of the newspapers. "Child Wonder in Finals Today." Child Wonder indeed! She was seventeen, wasn't she? Going on eighteen. "Gordon Favorite at Forest Hills Finals." Was she, though? She, Janet, would have something to say about that! She glanced over the account of the match in one paper and turned to Casey's column. Casey, the sportswriter, was always amusing, and she liked to read what he said even though she perceived that his knowledge of the game was sketchy.

"Tennis is a pretty uncertain thing and women's tennis is ten times as uncertain as men's, but ever since your servant turned his peepers on dainty little Janet Johnson three years ago at the Junior Championships in Cold Springs, he knew another tennis star was in the offing. Here she is today, ladies and gentlemen, in the place where Helen Moody and her rival Helen Jacobs and Alice Marble and others have made sporting history, and unless your correspondent is wrong this young lady will make some history in sport on her own before she steps down." Casey! Now . . . had Casey been at Cold Springs that first year? Janet was a literal young lady and believed what she saw in print. Casey . . . she was sure he hadn't been there. If so he hadn't paid her much attention. To be sure, she reflected, he had made up for this since. With a frown on her forehead she resumed his column. "Her match against Rosalind Kennedy, the Pacific Coast sensation, yesterday when the two youngsters battled almost two hours in a torrid sun, showed a large crowd at Forest Hills that this kid has the goods. She may not win this afternoon, but you can bet she'll make things hot for Irene. Another thing about Janet who just a year ago was a girl in pigtails batting her ball against a garage door in the suburbs . . ." I was not. I haven't worn pigtails for two . . . three . . . who told him that? "She's the easiest thing to watch in action since Kay Stammers of London used to display her wares over here. After some of the stolid matrons who consider it a sign of weakness to show their human side, if any, in public, Janet Johnson is a great relief. She likes to play, she enjoys herself when she's on court, and she isn't afraid to show it. Without a trace of affectation, this child really loves the game, and when she tosses back her head and laughs you know she means it. All in all, from my seat in Sec. 10, Row AA in the Stadium, she's about the most refreshing thing in tennis since high heels were forbidden on the court."

"Janet . . . Janet . . . lunch is ready, dear."

She threw down the newspaper and went into their sitting room. Useless to pretend this was an ordinary luncheon. Her parents did not so pretend; neither did Duncan Fletcher who came over from the Club to eat with them. One does not eat breakfast and lunch simultaneously every day in the year! She finished and went back to her bedroom to lie down for an hour, and then dress. When she rejoined them she was ready for the match. The ultimate touch was the yellow ribbon in her hair. This was Mrs. Johnson's idea. For every match Janet changed her color scheme. One day it was red, the next orange, then blue or yellow. Her tennis frock had a narrow yellow belt to match the bandeau, a small yellow handkerchief in a tiny pocket, and she wore yellow socks over her ankles. She was ready.

For some reason Janet's mother preferred to stay in the hotel. People walking through the square noticed Janet between the two older men; Duncan Fletcher, smart in white flannels and a white carnation in his buttonhole, carrying her racquets; on the other side her beloved, if rather shabby, dad.

"Why . . . that's . . . the young Johnson girl. She's the one in the finals today." They turned as the trio went past, for Janet was a picture. Her blonde hair matched the yellow in her costume, her face was flushed, and the white dress gathered attractively about her tall, graceful figure. Eager, excited, they moved toward the Club. Even the policeman on traffic duty in the Square looked back at the engaging youngster between the proud but serious men.

From the moment Janet descended the steps with Irene Gordon to face the packed Center Court, the whole thing passed in a kind of daze. She only remembered the kindly-faced umpire in his high chair calling:

"Miss Irene Gordon of Los Angeles . . . Miss Janet Johnson of New York . . . Miss Gordon will serve first." Then it was over. Like the flicker of a film; one minute she was down there in that heated pit looking up at the rows and rows of people in the stands, the next, hot and perspiring, she was gathering up her racquets by the umpire's chair. Her tennis-wise adversary realized the danger in the challenge, and determined never to permit Janet to get started. As those deep, long, and hard drives in the first game of all sent her stumbling and careening into the corners, Janet suddenly had a sensation of all-goneness somewhere under her heart. Usually her nervousness quickly disappeared in the heat of a contest, but that afternoon she was unable to get rid of a sinking feeling which deepened as the match progressed.

For the first time she was up against top-class stuff. Against a great player, against the real thing. She found that she was always reaching, that she was forever back on her heels instead of running forward to meet the ball. This was no girl to be worn down by accuracy and steadiness, nor yet to be beaten by speed, of which Janet now had plenty. When she hit to the far forehand corner with all her strength, the ball came back faster even than she had sent it. Harder and harder she tried, still the score mounted, still she was continually playing from her heels, something Chalmers had always warned her against. Yet save for that she wasn't playing badly, she wasn't making many mistakes. She was outclassed, that's all.

Mrs. Johnson sat before a radio in their sitting room at Forest Hills Inn, hating the announcer. At first he had been, so she felt, fair to Janet. Janet was the "young comer," the "brilliant youngster," the "crashing new sensation." To be sure, Irene Gordon was "the killer," and the "girl of the Golden West," and so on, but he spent more time on a description of her daughter and her daughter's history than on the champion. As the match went along, however, he devoted most of his lyricism to the champion and less to the pretender to the throne. Janet, whenever he mentioned her, was "in there trying every minute," and "making a plucky stand," but he failed to hide from the mother the fact that her daughter was not making a real battle. Notwithstanding his excited tones and his outbursts of emotion at what she felt were ordinary shots, it was evident that Janet was taking a first-class trimming. The applause which had been hearty at the start became perfunctory. The crowd had come to see the champion beaten. That's what crowds always come for, and to see the champion win again and win easily made them feel cheated.

". . . to the forehand corner, to the backhand by Irene and what a shot that was . . . now the kid comes back at her deep . . . Oh, boy, oh, boy . . . what a shot . . . what a shot . . . Irene hits to the backhand and comes in . . ." A burst of applause interrupted the speaker. "Yes, folks, you guessed it, Irene came in on the forehand, I mean the backhand, and once at the net made one of those wonderful volleys to win the point . . . yes, and game, too . . . making it four-two in the second set. First set to Miss Gordon, six games to one. While the two girls are at the umpire's chair drinking tea, we'll pause for station announcement."

Was it premonition or her mother's instinct which kept Mrs. Johnson from going to the finals? She never knew exactly. All she knew was that she couldn't bear to watch her child in distress. What had begun as a match of tennis ended as a debacle. It was soon over. She sat quietly in her rocker by the window overlooking the square, and when the contest finished, snapped off the radio. Soon a few persons appeared, hurrying from the arena to catch a train.

Other stragglers followed, an advance guard of the avalanche to come. Before long newsboys met them with complete accounts of the finals. From her window she could read the headlines.

"Gordon Beats Girl Wonder Easily." She rose, years older than when she had sat down forty minutes before. Janet would soon be back.

That evening, Janet lay on the bed crying. Mrs. Johnson, understanding and sympathetic, yet unable in the least to assuage the grief of youth, sat rocking beside the bed. Sobs racked the girl's body, the sobs of utter desolation. All the sweetness, all the exquisite savor of life which she had tasted so keenly the previous day, had vanished. She looked at life and there was no health in it. Twenty-four hours before she had been the wonder of the season, the sensation of the tournament, the champion of the future, admired, pointed out, photographed, talked about everywhere. Now she was nothing. Yes, she was, too; she was a failure, a false alarm. She had gone completely to pieces; she had cracked badly in her first real test.

Useless of her mother to repeat how well she had done to reach the finals, to beat Rosalind Kennedy and Grace Holdsworth, the English star, useless to comfort her, to suggest that she would do better next time as she had done against Rosalind. No, never, never, never would she play tennis again. She was a failure, she explained between sobs. A miserable failure. She was no good, never would be any good, never, at any time . . . and she hated it . . . hated it . . . hated it . . .

Her sobbing gradually became less unrestrained. Appreciating her daughter's distress, Mrs. Johnson was unable to help in the least. With her hand on the girl's still heaving shoulder, she began for the first time to have doubts about big-time tennis.

8

Pastures New

Yet two months made an enormous difference in Janet's attitude toward the game. That September evening after the finals she was convinced she would never again touch a racquet. But by mid-November the desire to prove herself—and to improve—had full possession of her soul. So Duncan Fletcher arranged some first-class coaching. Three times each week she journeyed to New York, and in an exclusive East Side tennis club with a good covered dirt court, she practiced with Robbins, the professional. Within a few months he had revolutionized her backhand, changed it from a poke to a stroke. Soon she began to hit it as freely as her forehand, and to enjoy hitting it, too. No longer did she have that instinctive dread of a hard ball on her left side. Teaching her to volley was more difficult, but before long she learned to put the ball away effectively if not gracefully. And he showed her how to smash gently from just behind the service line so an opponent could seldom reach the short return in time.

It was a winter of progress. Not fast or dazzling progress, and often for weeks she saw no change. Until all at once in a single afternoon she would play him a set and realize she was at last master of the backhand, afraid of nothing from the baseline no matter how hard he hit. She experimented, too, under his help and guidance, learning a slow dragged backhand shot sharply angled across court to pass an incoming volleyer. Then came the explosion.

The explosion merely stated that "New York is calling Mrs. William Johnson!" They were all seated in the living room one April evening when the telephone rang. It was answered by Mrs.

Johnson. The explosion could have been no more effective had it been a ten-inch gun.

"Yes . . . oh . . . oh, good evening, Mr. Fletcher. Yes . . . good evening . . . no . . . we hadn't heard . . . she is . . . oh, I see. . . . Oh, that's too bad . . . . I'm so sorry . . . Janet? . . . Well . . . I hardly know . . . I hardly think . . . I should certainly want to consider it very carefully . . . leaving school like that, Mr. Fletcher . . . her father and I . . . We'll think it over . . . yes. We'll let you hear from us tomorrow . . . Yes, I realize it would be a great opportunity for her. Yes . . . and when . . . when . . . Saturday? Yes, I'm sure it would be a fine thing . . . Thanks so much for thinking of her. We appreciate it lots . . . Thanks, Mr. Fletcher . . . Good night . . ."

"He wants you to go to Wimbledon . . . this very week!" Janet's heart jumped. How lucky she had been attentive and conscientious about her practice all winter, because the improvement in her game was quite as apparent to herself as to everyone else who watched her play. She was pleased most of all that she hadn't thrown up her game in discouragement. Wimbledon! To play at Wimbledon! It wasn't, it couldn't be, true. But it was true. Dorothy March, the third ranking player, was being married, the fourth ranking player was ill, and the fifth was in college and unable to leave. So Janet as a youngster with promise was next in line. It all depended on her mother. Her mother shook her head with distaste at any such odyssey.

"But why not, Mother? Why not? What difference does one month of school make? And Mrs. Sanderson is going, too. Why not, Mother? I'm almost twenty." Mrs. Johnson thought of Janet as a child of ten, a sweet, docile, and tractable child in a starched white dress and a large, floppy straw hat. Overnight, it seemed, this charming child had been transformed into a scowling, pleading, difficult young lady, and the transformation came as a shock to Mrs. Johnson.

The battle raged all that evening and much of the next day, but the outcome was never really uncertain. Reluctantly Mrs. Johnson granted permission. There were a hundred details to arrange and settle, new tennis dresses to be bought, a passport to be secured, bags to be packed, and every sort of unforeseen detail arising every hour that had to be settled. But somehow when the *Normandie* pulled out at noon that next Saturday, Janet, with Irene Gordon, Phyllis Dixon, the second ranking player, and Mrs. Sanderson, captain and manager of the team, was aboard. In her cabin on D deck was a sealed tin case with six racquets, delivered by special messenger that morning from the sporting goods manufacturers who made them. Janet was no longer using a single racquet. She was no longer paying for those she did use, either.

The next morning she was sitting alone in a chair on the promenade deck when he came past. It pulled her up short, brought her back home to the Old Center and the days of her childhood, and before she could stop she had called his name.

"Rodney!"

He turned and looked down at her. Tall, curly-haired, he came slowly toward her with the same half-diffident, half-confident manner as when, a boy in a blue suit at the party for the District Nurse Fund in Marchmont, he said, "I'm-sorry - I - pulled - yer - hair - c'mon - lemme - show - yer-the-turtles . . ."

He was the same old Rodney. If you knew Rodney Davis, you'd never forget him. But, anyway, forgetting him would have been difficult for

Janet because there had been far too many reminders of his progress through college. Once she had been taken by her father to a football game at New Haven and had seen him, a tiny figure in blue far below, the player of the afternoon in a tight-fought game. Rodney had been a favorite of sportswriters and radio men. As he sat beside her, older, boyish and yet not so boyish, she recalled half-forgotten phrases of some announcer floating into their living room at home.

"Fields and Davis now at ends for Yale . . . and Davis gets into the Princeton backfield and downs the man in his tracks . . . he's caught it . . . a pass to Davis . . . Yale nine, Princeton nothing . . ."

But that was over and done with. What was he doing now? He was in London. Yes, he had talked his father into giving him the English agency for a make of electric refrigerators in which the old man was interested. In three years he'd built up a temporary office into a regularly established branch of the main office with a corps of salesmen covering the British Isles. Like it? Yes, except the climate. Cold! Cold as the devil until you got used to it. Not now, not this time of the year? Yes, even this time of the year.

"I'll tell you." He leaned toward her and she noticed that when he talked he had the same ingratiating way, commanding and at the same time persuading, as when he had invited her to climb the tree. That had been her first sight of tennis. She watched him and, as she watched, began to understand his success in his job. "I'll tell you, Janet. Last June about the time of Wimbledon, I read a small item in the sports pages of the Times. Never forgot it either. It was during the big cricket matches against the Australians at Lords. It said," his eyes twinkled and his face lit up, "it said, 'There was a slight June frost on the cricket patch at Lords last night.' A slight June frost . . . get that? Wonderful, isn't it?"

H'm, yes, it was wonderful and then again it wasn't so funny either. She wanted terribly to get through one or two early rounds, to do something, win at least a match or two, because she knew her trip was an experiment on the part of the Tennis Association. One that wouldn't be repeated were she beaten early in the tournament. Yet to do well she needed warm weather and plenty of it. Janet was a warm-weather player; she thrived in heat.

Had he ever been to Wimbledon? Yes, it was some place, Wimbledon. Later in the trip it appeared he had also been to Forest Hills.

They were on deck one night after dancing in the Grand Salon. It was a warm evening, conducive to confidences, and Janet, finding someone who had met the test of sport and not failed as she had, knew he would understand. As they sat in their deck chairs, Casey the sports columnist passed them. He said good evening to the former junior champion, nodded casually to the one-time Yale end, and passed along.

"Somehow I don't trust that man Casey. Last year, the year before that is, he said I was a future champion. Mother has the clippings at home, lots of 'em. Then last summer he decides I'm no good, haven't the stamina to become a champion. A lot he knows! Just because I was beaten by Irene Gordon once. . . . She's beaten heaps of good players. . . ."

"Oh, he's all right, Casey is. Trouble is no one ever tells the truth to athletes. They either flatter 'em because they're winning or pan the stars out of 'em because they're losing. Now, as a matter of fact, you've got plenty of stamina. That isn't your trouble."

"What is my trouble?" Janet appealed with eagerness. Maybe he could help. "What is my trouble? I wish I knew. I play well enough, I beat people. Then every time I get into a really important match I seem to go to pieces, I don't do my best . . ."

"I know. I've been through it. You see I watched you closely last summer all through that tournament because I happened to be in New York at the time. What's more, I knew exactly what would happen when you played Gordon. Your first big fight, you were bound to tighten up. Always will until you get loose and easy in your big matches."

"Get loose? How do you mean?"

"Loose means . . . well, relaxed. Looseness comes partly from confidence. All the great athletes have it. Remember Kelley, played end at Yale before my time? He was always loose and free. That's your main trouble. You go on court, against players better than you are, as tight as a drum. All nerves; I watched you through glasses that afternoon—"

"Did you really?"

"Sure. I was awfully interested. But the minute you came out I knew you'd be beaten badly. You were just a bundle of nerves that afternoon."

"Uhuh. I certainly was. But how do you get—what is it—loose?"

"Darned if I know. It just comes from practice, and confidence, I suppose, in your ability. Why don't you try what I read this rookie on the Dodgers did, what's-his-name, Roy Tucker? Seems he was in a batting slump and all tightened up and things kept getting worse and worse, so every time he came to the plate he whistled. To himself, you know. . . ."

"Whistled?"

"Sure. It loosened him up. Relaxed his muscles. Try whistling yourself some time when you change courts. I remember I used to have the same trouble playing football at first, and I used to breathe deeply. That did the same thing. Then, well, there's another trouble with you. I'm no tennis player, but I know enough about the game to see one of your faults is you don't attack enough."

"Oh . . . Rodney!" Even Rodney. The same old complaint. "That's what everyone says to me. But I'm not a Californian. I didn't learn to play in California where they volley before they walk. I learned to play all by myself, against a garage door, and I learned to drive first of all, not to volley. Don't you understand?"

"Wait a minute. You have an attack just the same. It's your forehand drive, the greatest attacking shot in the game. That's your big gun. But you don't use it right. You try to bang these girls off the court. You can do it, too, against second-raters like Rosalind Kennedy, but you'll never do it against good players like Gordon. They're too sound."

"What must I do?"

"You must use your forehand to point up the attack, see? Then you must come to the net to finish the rally. You get a lot of defensive returns off even the best players, only you aren't in a position to take advantage of your forcing shot. Understand? You come in, yes, but you come in often at the wrong time . . . And when you come in, come right in . . ."

"Oh . . . I see. I think I understand." Janet had often been told this but never in words that were so clear. Numbers of people had advised her to volley, but never when to volley.

"Another thing. You ought to vary your strokes

much more, Janet. Your drives are always sound, but there's no variety in your game. Pull those girls in. Play a short one, then a long shot, then a fast one and a high one. Helen Moody was marvelous at changing pace. Vary your stroking. Now that shot where you run around your backhand and hit across court, that's a wonderful shot, but it's always hit at the same speed to the same spot. You must hit it down the line oftener. And come in behind it occasionally, see?" .

She saw. She saw much more than Rodney realized. She saw things she had noticed casually but never fully realized. She saw for the first time all the science and technique of what seemed like the simplest of ball games. She began to get under the surface of the thing called tennis, to appreciate why really good men are defeated by second-rate players. This game she had played so long and that she felt she knew so well, that she knew as an old friend, was really a stranger. But it opened up, it became familiar and understandable as he talked. Ah, why hadn't someone told her these things before?

" 'Nother thing, Janet, you've learned from professionals. You've never learned from anyone who has been through what you're going through.

There's one thing only an athlete . . . no, I don't mean that . . . only a competitor can tell you. Someone who's been out on that center court and seen a match already won fade from their grasp. That's pressure. When to apply pressure."

"When to what? I don't get you."

"It's like this. In any game between two teams and especially between two players evenly matched, there comes a critical moment of the contest. That's when one or the other is ready to crack. Now mind you, they don't always crack, unless pressure is applied. Sometimes the other man is just as tired, too tired to understand his moment has come, or maybe he doesn't know enough to apply pressure. You have to know when, to sort of feel it. Usually in football it's toward the end of the third quarter. In tennis— well, I'm not so sure when it is, probably never the same exact second. Maybe the last set, maybe sooner."

"Yes, but this pressure, how do you—what do you call it, apply . . ."

"That's your problem. You must put on pressure. Force the pace. Understand? Raise your game up, hit a little harder, come to the net a bit more, keep your opponent stretching for them . . . don't you see? You make your opponent play just a little better to keep up with you."

"I see, I see. Oh, Rodney, if only I had you up somewhere in the stands telling me when to hit, when to force the pace . . ."

He leaned over and laid a paw on her arm. "It's a bet, Kid. I'll be there at Wimbledon every time you play an important match next week."

9

Wimbledon

No doubt about it, Wimbledon was different.
Forest Hills was a man's show. The men's
finals was the important match. The men players
were always the best stars of the tennis world,
they were the attraction for which the crowd
came. Wimbledon on the other hand was a woman's tournament. Janet was struck immediately
by the preponderance of women in the gallery.
It appeared that, in England anyway, women
preferred to watch women playing tennis. Moreover dressing for the part interested them in-

tensely; the magazines and newspapers were full of pictures of the girl players and descriptions of their clothes: shorts, skirts, divided skirts, caps, no caps, visors, no visors, bandeaus or none, tennis frocks or two-piecers, all the trappings of the game were discussed on every hand.

What a cosmopolitan place Wimbledon was, too. The dressing rooms were jammed with a dozen nationalities jabbering in a dozen different tongues: coffee-skinned maids from India and Jamaica, laughing French girls, blonde Scandinavians, sturdy-legged Britishers, slanty-eyed Chinese, as well as players from the Argentine, South Africa, and other distant parts of the earth that were merely names in geography to Janet. It was all new; a new world, vivid, exciting, and she looked forward eagerly to the tournament about to begin.

Her first match was scheduled on one of the far outer courts, hidden by high hedges from the milling throng of spectators. One of the ordinary outer courts, but what a court it was! Hard as a board, smooth, perfect turf, the kind of turf only England can produce. A court inferior, she presumed, to the best at Wimbledon, yet better far than anything she had ever played upon, even the center court at Forest Hills. When she appeared, there at one side leaning over the green baize barrier was Rodney, true to his promise on the boat.

Janet was tall, but her blonde opponent was taller. Greta Fischel had long legs and long arms, and as they rallied before the match she looked like a kind of spider, a resemblance heightened by her awkward strokes and her manner of snatching at the ball as if she were catching a fly. Janet smiled across to Rodney. This was easy. At least she'd get past one round.

For the German girl had nothing. She clung tenaciously to the baseline, scuttling hastily backward whenever she was drawn in. Hitting the ball with a clumsy push, her only good shot was an accurate, deep forehand drive. Janet was carelessly confident, and with poised strokes won the first three games. Then she became inattentive, and before she realized it had lost three games and the score was even. She tried to concentrate but things didn't come off; in a few minutes the set was gone. She paused by Rodney, wiping her face with a towel. Casey, the sportswriter, stood behind him, watching indifferently.

Rodney leaned toward her. "Look here, baby, that gal's better than she looks. You'll have to hit harder, you softened up completely toward the end of that set." But the persistent German, covering court beautifully, seemed to have an answer for everything. To beat her took a really first-class shot. True, she had no backhand, but her agility was so great she ran around everything on the left and struck the ball with her forehand. Aha, my old trick, thought Janet, and maneuvering carefully she hit down the left side and came to the net. To her astonishment the girl passed her with a deceptively slow but accurate drive off the backhand.

"Games four-three, Fräulein Fischel leads, second set," mumbled the umpire. A panicky feeling overcame Janet. Two games from defeat! In her first match, too. Beaten by an unknown German girl in the opening round. She saw Rodney beckoning.

"Janet! Get hold of yourself. Take a good deep breath. Now another. Now whistle . . . well . . . try it . . . that's fine. Relax. You're all tightened up. Now go out and hit that ball; you've been pushing it all this set . . . ."

"Yes . . . but, Rod . . . she's so . . . so awfully steady . . . she never misses . . ." panted Janet.

"Sure she's steady. Because you never force

her. You give her what she wants. You can't out-steady her. You must hit wide to her right. . . ."

"Why . . . that's her best shot."

"But it always comes the same place across court. Haven't you noticed?" Angry, hot, discouraged, Janet felt like kicking herself. Once more in the face of defeat she had lost control of her thinking apparatus. Rodney continued, "When you have her way out on the right, crack the ball straight down the line to her backhand and come in. Come to the net. Now relax . . . go out and hit that ball on the nose."

Janet tried it. The first time, her forehand down the line left the other girl standing on the opposite side of the court. The second time, the German reached the ball, but the reply was weak and Janet at the net put it away. Rodney was right, that forehand invariably came from left to right. Why, oh, why didn't she keep her head and see things like that? Would she ever learn? . . . Soon she had won the game. Now the German was worried, perspiring, blown, and less sure of herself. That backhand poke, so steady and safe when she had time, was a flubbed stroke when she was forced to run for it. She made a couple of errors and a few minutes later Janet had won the second set.

The third set was a battle. That pertinacious spider, handicapped as she was with inferior weapons, had courage and grit. She fought valiantly against Janet's polished strokes. She was reaching everything with her long legs and arms, and as the set progressed there was nothing to tell who would win. Never more than a game separated them, and the strain began to tell on Janet as she gradually realized she was in a struggle for her very life, a struggle in which nothing but her best game would pull through.

"If . . . this . . . is what you get the first round . . ." she panted in Rodney's ear as her opponent stopped for a minute at the umpire's chair to fix her hair, "what'll . . . the next ones be like?"

"Quit thinking about the next ones. Concentrate on this match, baby."

Several games later she came toward him. She had broken the German's service and was leading at last, four games to three. "Rodney, I'm dying. Get me a Coke, please."

He shook his head. "Well, then a glass of water . . . anything . . . something to drink."

"You're okay. You keep right on as you're going. You're playing a winning game."

"Yes, but I need a drink. I must have one."

"You go on playing," said the relentless Rodney. And Janet went on drinkless to the end.

As she returned triumphantly to the dressing room, she heard shouts from the center court and noticed people rushing past her. "Phyllis Dixon, the American, is being badly beaten by that French girl," someone called. Janet looked up at the electric scoreboard on the promenade. Yes, Phyllis was behind a set, and one-four down in the second. Half an hour later a disappointed girl joined Janet in the dressing room. The American delegation had been reduced to herself and Irene Gordon.

But with every match Janet gained confidence. The weather grew warmer, not hot, but at least sunny and warm. Janet's weather. The firm, true turf with never a single bad bounce, with the perfect green background, suited her game. She liked it, liked, too, the friendly crowds who had adopted her and began following her from court to court in different matches. It was a great fortnight.

Toward the end of that fortnight, Casey, the sportswriter, sat in the press room, his typewriter before him, engaged in the most difficult of all tasks, eating his words. He flipped a match to the floor and remarked to the man next to him, "Well, can you beat it? I'm gonna stop guessing about women's tennis from now on." With disgust he started on his evening story for New York.

"Irene Gordon, American champion and three times winner at Wimbledon, unexpectedly went down to defeat today before the amazing game of Germaine Saulnier, French titleholder and brilliant young continental star, whom oldtimers here at Wimbledon compare to the great Suzanne Lenglen. The score was 8–6, 6–2, and . . ." Casey went on for several paragraphs before he began that dismal process of masticating his words. It had to come.

"So here we are with little Janet Johnson, the only American left in the tournament, facing Mlle. Saulnier in the finals tomorrow. As one who makes more than his share of mistakes, let me say you could have had 20 to 1 against Janet reaching the finals, and in fact that's exactly what the quoted odds were here in London two weeks ago. With all our men players beaten, with Irene Gordon out, this little Cinderella, who was sent along because no one else wanted to come, remains the only American left at Wimbledon. I saw Janet on the opening day manhandled by a raw-boned Fräulein who is said to be a cross-country champion from Munich, and certainly looked the part. When I left their court the American girl was cracking wide open, and when I returned half an hour later she was coming off victorious. She's got better and more confident with every match, and the way she swings that forehand across court makes your servant think of Helen Moody at her best. Win? No, she hasn't any chance against a more experienced opponent who was good enough to take Irene Gordon without the loss of a set, but as one who all along has been saying Janet didn't have the goods and was only a pretty young girl in a white dress adding to the scenery, this cynic wishes to put himself right and admit . . ."

10

Turn in the Tide

They clustered about her in the dressing room; Mrs. Sanderson the captain, the girls; several attendants fluttering around while she dressed. Scared? No. Why should she be? She couldn't hope to beat a girl who'd beaten Irene, so the job was easy. Just go out and do her darnedest. That's what she proposed doing, too. What if the Queen were there? Made no difference to her. In fact Janet never felt more like playing tennis. The day was really hot, the kind of weather she thrived on. Nobody expected her to win so there wasn't any tenseness in her attitude. Then there was her dress, her best dress, her favorite dress. She looked well in it, she always played well in it . . . are they ready . . .

"All ready for you now, Miss Johnson."

As they stepped onto the Centre Court to ripples of applause, a barrage of photographers, one row kneeling and a semicircle standing behind them, greeted the two girls. Compared to the sturdy, older French girl, Janet seemed younger than her twenty years. Her simple white piqué dress accentuated her youthfulness. It had a small rounded collar buttoned close to the throat and was sleeveless, coming just over her shoulders but slit to permit her to reach for a smash or a high service without raising the dress as she moved. The blouse was plain and from the pocket showed the corner of a yellow handkerchief. Her socks were yellow and her dress was caught loosely round the waist by a yellow belt, while she wore a ribbon of a slightly darker shade that matched her hair. Her circular skirt reaching just below her knees swished gracefully as she moved up to the waiting umpire who stood beside his chair, scorepad in hand. Beside that worldly and poised adversary she was charmingly fresh and unspoiled. Although Janet did not realize it for many years, on her appearance that afternoon she had captured the most valuable asset the Centre Court can bestow: the favor of the Wimbledon gallery.

If the outer courts had been good, this one save for the worn patch at the baseline was perfect. She leaned into her drives with all the force of her body, meeting the ball with accurate timing and sending it skimming like a bird across the net. Somehow she felt as lighthearted as light-footed, she was exhilarated and inspired; by the Queen in the Royal Box behind her, by the thousands jammed into the big arena, the sunshine overhead, the importance of the occasion. While they rallied she could hear little murmurs of approval from the spectators in the front row close to the court. There was no restraint, no hesitation in her shots, and when the match began her command of the ball grew. Everything she tried was successful. Service aces down the center line, half volleys, smashes, and passing shots flowed in an endless stream from her racquet, and thunders of noise greeted every winning shot. The vast gallery packed to the distant reaches of the roof was in at the birth of a champion; they were watching sporting history in the making. Tennis-wise, they realized it and gave their accolade to her progress on the firm green turf below.

". . . AND the first set to Miss Johnson, six games to two . . ." The elderly umpire clambered down from his perch to measure the net, while the two girls paused a moment to wipe their faces. A hum rose over the assemblage. "What a player . . . not a Californian . . . no . . . they say she comes from the East . . . wonderful . . . yes, marvelous the way she conceals that forehand . . . ever see anything like . . ."

But that French girl was of peasant stock; born with all the courage and determination of France in her blood; strong, not easily subdued. Conqueror of many championships, she realized she had youth to deal with, and youth could be, must be, upset. So she proceeded to try her best to accomplish that aim.

Her first task was to slow down the tempo of the game; the whole game, not merely her opponent's strokes but her thinking process and her reflexes also. She stopped to tie her shoes between rallies, she remained at the umpire's chair toweling her face while Janet stood impatiently on the baseline waiting to serve. She annoyed her young opponent in every way possible, dragging about the court between rallies, slouching to the service line with hesitating steps. It was war—war with no rules, but war, and she was in there to win. To win she had to break the cadence of Janet's game, to do this she brought her cunning into action; now a drop shot, now a slow, high, lofted shot to the baseline that bounced round Janet's shoulder, now a cut that had her reaching into the turf. It was an irritating, teasing, upsetting game, a game that had won many a victory, a game calculated to upset an inexperienced youngster who hit hard and frankly. There was nothing that could really be stroked. Janet faltered as Irene Gordon had faltered the previous day; who wouldn't before such tactics? With victory in her hands, she wavered, hesitated in her stroking, became tentative and lost command of the court.

"Second set to Mademoiselle Saulnier, six games to three."

There was no rest at Wimbledon after the second set. As Janet paused momentarily at the umpire's chair, sipping some tea, she heard comments from those seated near in the hum that rose round the enclosure. "Yes . . . couldn't quite do it . . . a bit too young, eh . . . what a pity . . . needs a little more . . . ought never to have dropped that set . . ."

Now then! Rodney! Where was he? Rod would tell her what to do, signal how to play that last set. Because she had a chance to win, she knew she had a chance. Think of it, a chance to become Wimbledon champion! She wasn't beaten yet, no siree! Eagerly she looked round the front benches, at the rows and rows of faces, men and women attentively leaning on the rail and peering down at her. But nowhere any answering smile, any signal, any Rodney, nowhere . . .

They went back on court. The crowd applauded and settled back for the kill. In what seemed only a minute she heard the umpire's voice through his mike. "Games are three-love, Mademoiselle Saulnier leads, third set . . ."

Janet was upset, worried now, completely thrown off her stride as she had been in that first match against the German girl. Her game was disintegrating as it had done the first day, taken apart under the pressure of insidious shots sent over by the crafty French player. Suddenly she perceived that tennis was not really a contest of strokes at all, but a contest of character. Of will against will, of one player trying to break down the will of another. This girl had no weakness like the Fräulein, either. Janet paused as she started to serve, and fumbling with her hair for a moment attempted to collect herself. What was it Rodney had said? Breathe deeply. Relax. Hit, hit, hit out.

"You know, I could have sworn I heard her whistling to herself that third set," one linesman remarked to the other after the match.

That little respite enabled her to get a grip on her fading faculties. She must hit, hit out. If she were to be beaten, at least she could go down fighting. The ball came slightly to her left side, and stepping deftly round it, she struck it with her forehand as hard as she could. It went low across court and deep into the backhand corner. The French girl reached, lunged, missed. Applause from the crowd that all through the set had been strangely silent. They wanted Janet to win.

In the next rally she got another slow ball to the left, and running round it again smacked a

terrific drive straight down the line. Her opponent, balancing on the baseline, turned, stretched
for the ball, and sent back a high, feeble return.
Now . . . now . . . now . . . careful . . . watch
the ball. Janet closed in while the French girl
danced on her toes far behind the baseline to
return the expected smash. Then Janet remembered. The slow return, that short smash she
had been taught! It was daring, it was taking a
chance, but . . . and she tapped the ball with
a firm hand and arm. It fell over the net inside
the service line while her opponent stood help-
lessly far away. The stands rocked with applause. Beyond the baseline the French girl shook
her head, hand on hip, her breast heaving, and
a look of sudden despair on her face. It was an
electric shock to Janet. Instantly she recalled
what Rodney had told her on the boat.

Pressure. There was always a time . . . in
every game . . . in every match . . . the third
quarter . . . end of the third quarter . . . press
her . . . press. Press . . . That was the thing.
Yes, this was the big moment. Forgetting the
crowd, the score, the importance of every point
and every stroke, she threw her youth into the
scale. Hitting firmly, she ran her tired adversary
with low, strong drives from side to side, fast,

faster, deep shots that had the French girl backing up to return them, now plunging to one corner or the other. The rally was everlasting, each player realizing the importance of the game. One-three or four-love; a game on which the match might depend. Fencing with care, Janet suddenly lashed out with all her strength and came to the net. A clean volley into unprotected territory, and once again that spontaneous burst of noise, once again the despairing look on the face of the other girl.

". . . and games are three-one, Mademoiselle Saulnier leads, third set." Janet tossed the two balls in her hand over the net with confidence. If only she could keep up the pressure.

Now the French player was worried. She saw the danger. She was tired. She was older and not nearly so fresh as Janet because she had been doing much more chasing. At the start she had been blown off the court, had pulled herself out of the hole by clever tactics, and now that young amazon was snatching the game from her hands. She had tried everything and her best wasn't good enough to stem that hailstorm of drives and volleys which, stirred by the thunder of applause, kept raining into court.

The applause was echoed and re-echoed by

the crowd on the outer promenade who were watching the match from the big electric scoreboard. They also wanted Janet to win. At that critical moment, all this told. It gave her added strength and courage. She began hitting the target with every stroke, nicking the corners with deep fast drives, and the French girl became a worried bungler, feebly attempting to stem the incoming tide. The gallery was in ecstasy at the surge of their favorite. Could she keep that pace up? Yes, she got better as she went on, while the other's defense wavered, crumbled, broke completely. . . .

". . . set AND match, Miss Johnson. . . ."

His words were drowned in a mighty shout, a most un-English yell of delight as Janet rushed to the net to shake a limp and perspiring hand. She felt she could have gone on playing like that forever.

The photographers assaulted them as they gathered their racquets and moved toward the dressing room. Janet flushed, triumphant, the French player beside her expostulating, explaining, disappointed, shrugging her shoulders, in no good humor. Elderly officials pushed near, trying to shake Janet's hand. In the front rows close to the ground the spectators stood applauding as they walked off the court, showering her with cheering words. Together they moved under the British Broadcasting booth to the dressing room.

And there in the doorway stood—Rodney!

It wasn't until later that she discovered how he had worked to get into that particular holy of holies at that particular moment; how he had bribed attendants, explained to officials, shoved past players waiting to take the court, and so to the very entrance itself where he stood when she came off. His arms were open. He kissed her, and Janet liked it.

"Rod Davis! Where were you? You promised . . . you said you'd . . ."

"Right there, honey, right in the stands all the time. But I decided to let you play your own match and find yourself in your own way. Only I didn't realize you'd do it like this . . . Janet . . . it was wonderful. . . . I'm proud of you. . . ."

11

Champion Off Duty

Janet was changing. During those next twelve months in which she gradually pulled herself to a position where she dominated the world of woman's tennis on two continents, many things happened. There was also the change in the relations with her mother. Mrs. Johnson still traveled along with Janet, still went round the circuit in summer, from Seabright to Southampton to Forest Hills. Outwardly they were as devoted and united as when Janet had been a child prodigy at Cold Springs with hair down her back and a sailor blouse. But the champion now ran her own show.

The fact was that the several years of exacting discipline necessary to master a sport such as tennis, plus the struggle in big matches with the keenest brains in the game, brains that had to be subdued and mastered before their possessors were worsted physically, all this had left its mark on Janet. It had perforce taught her stern and bitter lessons. You can't develop willpower without developing willpower. Whereas she had been strangely young and immature a year and a half before, now she was the opposite. Her tennis had aged her tremendously, given her character as well as maturity and knowledge. Before long she knew the men and policies of the Tennis Association quite as fully as anyone, and she kept a firm hand on her worldly affairs. She perceived that all top-class players were attached to one or another sporting goods house; performed with the racquets and equipment of that firm, played especially in tournaments where the firm's balls were used, and received a salary for so doing. The Tennis Association was aware of the fact that she was on the payroll of Morrisons, Inc., but they took good care not to mention the matter to her, and Janet knew enough to keep it to herself.

The sudden death of her father of heart disease late that spring had canceled her trip to defend her title at Wimbledon; a title she would easily have won had she been there. By mid-August she was staying with her mother in a big New York hotel, the fortnight before the championships at Forest Hills. One hot afternoon the telephone jangled and a voice announced that Mr. Rodney Davis was downstairs to see Miss Johnson.

Rodney Davis! For once Janet was rocked. She was in the middle of one of the busiest afternoons of the summer, and of all persons he was the last she expected to see. Must be on a quick business trip. All right, send him up.

"Rodney . . . Rod Davis . . ." she called to her astonished parent as she scuttled into the bedroom, leaving her mother to greet him. It was more than a year since she had left him rather tremulously on the platform of Waterloo Station in London, and the letters she had received told nothing of this unexpected visit. When she appeared, she had changed her dress for a flowered print, one of her most becoming creations. Rod didn't know this; her mother did.

She was busy, she was rushed, she had a million things to do, but she was delighted to see him. Really delighted, and her face showed it. "Well, well . . . how glad I am to see you . . . same old Rod," said Janet as if she meant it, and she did mean it. Rodney looked at her queerly, this strange, beautiful, grown-up person who suddenly filled the room with her personality. Her hair, he noticed, was done differently, her manner and her clothes and her whole appearance were those of quite another person from the sparklingly fresh young girl of Wimbledon's Centre Court. He was pleased to see her, too, but he couldn't echo her words. She certainly wasn't the same. Attractive still, perhaps even more so, but changed she certainly had. Lots, he thought.

How'd he leave London? Good . . . No, she couldn't get across. Her dear father . . . yes, he'd heard. Next year, maybe. Was he home for long? How was business? Rod wasn't exactly sure about things. He was a trifle bewildered by her clothes and her coiffure and her perfume and her general air, a kind of allure which made her a totally different person, another Janet entirely. She kept peppering him with queries. Would he be round for the Nationals next month? Rod was still vague. He might, then again . . .

The telephone jangled. He noticed a change in her voice, too, as she talked, even her voice was firmer and more mature. "Oooh, Mr. Dudley! It's so good of you to call . . . yes . . . yes, well, there're so many things I need your advice about . . ." Rats, thought Rodney to himself. That young lady doesn't need advice from anybody. "What's that? California? Oooh, I don't know. I might possibly go out to their Southwest tournament next month, then on the other hand . . . Oh, I see. Well, that's different then. I understand. Why don't you run up to the hotel this afternoon and we'll talk things over. No, I practiced this morning. About six? That'll be fine. Good-bye . . ."

She replaced the instrument. Almost immediately the bell of the door of the suite jingled and her mother rose and went to the door in the hall. She returned. "It's that girl from the *Daily Mail*, Janet. You have an appointment for an interview at three-thirty."

Janet looked at her wristwatch impatiently.

Rodney stood up to go, but she grabbed his arm. "Sit down!" There was command in her tone and force in her gesture. Rodney sat down. "I have to spend my life nowadays with people I don't like, and it's not often I get a chance to be with someone I do like. This won't take long. You and I are going to have dinner together. Wait until I get rid of this girl. It won't take long. They ought to send a man, I hate girls. They look you all over, your clothes and everything." She glanced at herself in the mirror, and then went to the door. "Won't you come in, please."

While Rodney, astride a chair, was watching the scene with a queer expression on those closed lips, the young woman reporter jumped into the interview. Yes, Janet could certainly handle herself all right in a broken field. She had changed, undoubtedly. Between questions the reporter sipped a glass of light sherry. Sherry, thought Rodney, the acceptable drink, the correct apéritif. It was plain Janet knew her way about town.

While the champion was talking, the girl was taking notes on the back of an envelope, at the same time making a rapid but accurate sketch of the way she did her hair, and the dress she was wearing, because the photographer in the hall outside might miss those details. She knew what Rodney didn't: that the dress was a Chenard model. It must be true what everyone said, that champions got their clothes for nothing. The woman that was in the reporter wondered to herself why she hadn't gone in for sport instead of the business of writing.

Janet continued. "Engaged? To whom? To Benny Fishman, the orchestra leader!" She threw back her head and laughed. Aha, thought Rodney, so that's it, is it? "Oh, heavens, no. We're just friends, that's all. I adore him, but we're only good friends. What's that? The new president of the Tennis Association?" Now she became serious. Her smile faded. "Ooooh, are you sure? You heard . . . you did . . . are you quite sure? No, I hadn't heard about it myself. Yes, I know Mr. Dudley quite well. But you won't put this in the paper, will you? Mr. Fletcher was such a lovely man. But Mr. Dudley, well, he's more progressive, if you know what I mean? Not that I don't get on with Mr. Fletcher; please don't think that. We're old friends; he's been terribly kind to Mother and me. Hasn't he, Mother? We . . . I owe him a great deal. But I do admire progressive people, don't you? What's that? A message to the girls of America? H'm . . . well, tell them to play fair, not to take games too seriously, to win or lose with a smile. That's the lesson sport teaches us. Must you go? Oh . . . what a nice interview. It's been lots of fun. Be sure and come up when you see me again, I meet so many newspaper people nowadays . . . Good-bye . . . good-bye . . ."

The door closed. The champion sank into a chair beside her guest, who was looking at her quizzically.

"Mother," said Janet, "Mother, would you please get Mr. Dudley for me on the telephone? At the Association. No, call and ask him . . . tell him I've got a visitor from London just here and could he manage to come up at five instead of six . . ."

12

Rodney in Trouble

Six weeks later Rodney sat halfway up the
Stadium at Forest Hills on a steaming hot
afternoon in September. Janet was playing a
quarter-finals match and although she could easily have placed him in one of the front boxes
under the marquee at the side of the court, he
preferred to sit in the stands and listen to the
comments of the crowd. Besides he knew the
only place to watch tennis is back of the court,
not from a box beside the net.

He glanced around as the two players took the court. Just in front of him three young girls were chattering to each other. "Yes, they say her father really taught her . . . I suppose she has had a lot of coaching, too, don't you, Helen? I think she's adorable, isn't she? Uhuh, not really like a tennis champion, somehow. Most players haven't nice legs, have they? Betty's are thick, and Eileen's are sort of funny, and Jessie has bow legs, and Florence's are wonky. But Janet has lovely legs. Did you see her beat Florence yesterday?"

Behind him was a conversation of a different sort. "My dear, I believe they're quite ordinary people, from some little town up in Massachusetts originally, so Jim says. He knows them well, that is, he's met them, the mother and girl. He's a friend of Duncan Fletcher who's something or other in the Tennis Association. That's him now, see . . . down there standing near the net in tennis flannels. Yes, it seems they're just nice country people and the girl had a flair for the game. Oh, George! Look at that. Did you see that last shot she made?"

Down on the court the umpire was climbing slowly into his high chair. Duncan Fletcher, very smart in his white flannels and fawn-colored jacket with a badge prominently displayed on the pocket, was shooing a battalion of cameramen and movie operators toward the exit. From the stands it appeared that the last word was with the cameramen.

Rodney watched Janet standing on the baseline ready to serve, a cool, competent young lady, apparently not at all worried about the match ahead. In fact he had seen her the previous evening and knew she was not worried. He wondered whether others beside himself noticed the difference in Janet, the change in her demeanor, the ease and freedom of her stroking, the calm confidence in her manner. Fourteen months before at Wimbledon she had been a girl; now she was a woman. She had lost the immature gawkiness of youth, her figure was fuller, more graceful. Her muscular coordination was beautiful to watch. She was always completely sure of herself, perfectly balanced, never at a loss for the exact move or the precise shot which the situation demanded. As champion she no longer had that wistful appeal; like her figure, her game and her character, he observed, had solidified. The difference was plain as she stood tapping a ball with her racquet, waiting for the command of the umpire to begin play. That gentleman settled himself fussily into his chair, arranged the scoreboard to his satisfaction, straightened the microphone before his face, looked round to see that the linesmen were in place, and then droned forth the magic order.

"Miss Janet Johnson of New York . . . Miss Myrtle Robbins of California. . . . Miss Johnson will serve first . . . linesmen ready . . . play. . . ."

Five hours later Rodney sat with the victor of the afternoon on the terrace of the clubhouse. There was a dance within at which she permitted herself the luxury of appearing for a little while. It was one of the obligations of being a champion, for if she didn't appear, people said she was stuck-up. Of course she never stayed late, no one in training can afford late hours, and Janet in diet and regime still submitted to her mother. Inside a band thummed and strummed; before them stretched the empty courts in the moonlight. For the first time Rodney was explaining the reasons for his return from England and his trouble since his arrival in New York.

"You see, when the English placed that tariff on imported refrigerators last year, it just about killed our business. In six months the bottom had . . ."

"How do you mean? They wouldn't let you import any more from this side?"

"Oh, they'd let us import all right. But the duty was so high it made them more expensive than English refrigerators and those American ones built in factories over there. As it was, the business fell away to nothing. It practically killed the branch in six months, so I had to come home. Nothing else to do."

"But, Rod, surely there's room for you over here, in the main office in New York or somewhere?"

"You'd have thought so, wouldn't you?" His reply was bitter. "For a man who built a branch from nothing to a total of half a million dollars' worth of business a year. Well, you see foreign managers are seldom overpopular with the home office. 'Nother thing, the company really couldn't do much for me. They were going through what the boys call a reorganization. When I got back I found our branch was one of the few profitable branches they had last year. Rather, up to last year."

"But the mills, Rodney? The mills up home." To Janet the Davises were still the owners of the big mills in the village, lords of Marchmont, drivers of Packards, squires of the town and county. She forgot that years had passed and that many things had changed since she left the hill and the Old Center.

"The mills! Huh. Why, the cotton business up there practically disappeared five years ago. That's why Father put me into this line. He saw it coming; he knew the cotton business was washed up in New England. The mills failed the year after Father's death. We didn't have the word reorganization in our vocabulary then. I'm glad he didn't live to see it."

Now Janet was silent. She was genuinely shocked. The Davises in trouble. It seemed incredible. "But surely, Rod," she said after a minute's hesitation, "surely there must be lots of things you could do. Lots of businesses that'd be glad of someone with your experience?"

"Yeah. That's what I figured three months ago. But these last weeks haven't been pleasant. You see, Janet, I've lost all my connections, being away so long from home. Folks forget you awful fast. Then again no one wants a man who's run his own show. And they're cutting down.

They want to get people cheap. Now if I was just out of college and starting in, that would be a different matter."

"Poor Rodney." She put her hand over his. A feeling of remorse came upon her. In the past weeks they had been much together and she had bothered him constantly with her troubles, the troubles of a champion. Troubles which were real enough to Janet, but compared to his they seemed pretty trivial.

Rodney Davis out of a job! Why, it was simply unbelievable. It was monstrous. He squeezed her hand. She looked at him, attractive in a white dinner coat. He squeezed her hand again. Then he spoke.

"You know before all this happened, last winter, I mean, I sort of hoped I'd be able to come over and take you back with me. To London, away from all . . ." He waved his hands over the turf which smelt damp and fresh in the fall evening. "Away from tennis, from that . . ." He gestured toward the white mass of the stadium, gaunt in the moonlight beyond.

Janet instantly withdrew her hands. Her back straightened. "Why? What's the matter with tennis?"

"Oh, nothing, my dear. Nothing the matter

with tennis at all. Don't misunderstand me. It's the champion business and how it affects people I'm thinking about. Sure, I'll be out there in the stadium pulling for you tomorrow, and Saturday in the finals. It isn't that at all, it's the way big time competition seems to harden everyone. To be tops in sport nowadays means you have to devote your whole life to it; seems to do something to a person, to those who . . ."

Janet sniffed. She was indignant. Her sympathy for his jobless state, which had been so alive but a minute previously, died. "But that's just it. I don't. I don't devote my whole life to tennis. Actually I play very little. Less all the time. That's horrid of you, Rodney. Why, I have lots of things beside sport, lots . . ."

He hooted. Not a nice polite laugh, but a derisive snort. "Skip it. You aren't talking to Casey or that gal from the *Mail*. You know perfectly well what I mean. Do you want to . . . Look here. Janet, if you don't watch out, some day you'll stop being a woman and become a tennis champion. I can see the change in you already in the last few years, no one can be in this hard-boiled atmosphere and not change. Don't you see where it leads?"

Janet stopped him with a gesture. This wasn't

at all the kind of thing to which she was accustomed. Duncan Fletcher never talked to her like that, neither did Mr. Dudley, nor any of the umpires, nor in fact the other officials. No, nor the sportswriters who gathered about her in the clubhouse lounge after a match for an interview with the champion. Her real friends never talked that way, either. And on the eve of her big match of the year, too. It was tactless. It was positively unkind. None of her friends would have done such a thing. Not at all. "Your game was *simply* marvelous today, Janet . . . never saw you play better, my dear. . . . You were *simply* wonderful in that second set this afternoon. . . . Did you see that article about you in the *Evening Mail*, Miss Johnson?"

No. She didn't care for his attitude. Doing things to her! What did that mean, anyway? He was presuming because he'd known her so long.

"I must say you didn't grow complimentary while you were in England, did you? I've always heard Englishmen weren't very flattering to their women; must be catching. Why, Rod, you used to be such a help to me, I'll never forget how you pulled me through my first match at Wimbledon. You never used to say nasty things to me in those days."

"You weren't champion then, my dear."

"What difference does that make? And I . . . I mean I really don't feel there's much danger . . ."

Rodney looked down at her in the moonlight. A Chenard dinner dress showed her lovely throat and shoulders, and her firm, round arms. She was beautiful, and she knew she was beautiful. But he continued.

"Aha! Yes, you think so right now. You don't realize what you'll become if you give yourself up entirely to sport."

"Oh, *Rodney!*" This was too thick. But he stuck to it.

"Being champion means fighting off the youngsters, killing the challengers, working, practicing, sacrificing your existence to tennis and the champion business. You have to be tough on the court, yes, and tougher all the time. You get to be insincere—I was listening to that newspaper interview the other day. A champion has to play cleverly, on the court and off, and it's mighty hard to stay sweet and natural under that pressure."

"Rodney! I think that's perfectly hateful."

"Maybe. You don't like to hear it. You can't stand facing up to things. But you get the point."

By this time Janet was thoroughly angry, and she knew he was the one person alive who could make her angry. What she would have said, what reply she would have made to all this, she never really knew. She was saved by an interruption. From the porch behind came a voice.

"Janet! Janet! Is that you, dear?"

She jumped up. "Yes, Mother. I'll be right in."

"Ten o'clock, dearie. Time to go home."

Time to go home. Time to go home, imitated Rodney. To himself, however. He knew when Janet was upset and annoyed.

She went in, saying good-bye. One of the bores of being champion was trying to appear at these functions as if one had had a really pleasant evening, as if one had enjoyed oneself. Janet hadn't enjoyed herself in the least. Her face was scowling, it was flushed and had a strangely un-Janetlike appearance; anything but the composed face of the champion of the Center Court. She was only glad to get away, and she had some difficulty in keeping that fact concealed from the throng in the room. She was in training, she couldn't stay. How fortunate . . . that it was time to leave.

13

The Champion Meets a Test

There comes a time in the course of human events when the champion suddenly feels herself losing her grip on life. When even the salt of competition and the excitement of tournament play begin to lose their flavor. It came the following summer when, after having won the title three times, the chief interest of the sporting public was seeing who could unseat Janet from her throne. This feeling comes into the life of every great champion, but she did not appreciate that. Nor would it have consoled her greatly if she had. Things were not going properly.

First of all there was Rodney. He never came to see her play, or rather he came only on rare days. To be sure, he had a job and could seldom get away, but his attitude was distinctly not helpful. He seemed to have no understanding of and no sympathy for the problems she faced. Then there was the strange attitude of the tennis galleries. For whereas Janet had once been a talented and charming little girl, a possibility of the future, she was now exactly the opposite. She was champion; by no means devoid of grace and charm in action, but devoid of uncertainty. She was winning as she had won for several years with a regularity that was becoming monotonous. "What's the use of going down to Forest Hills today?" people said. "Johnson's sure to win. It's in the bag."

What more natural, therefore, that she should find the crowd somewhat apathetic to her best shots, that they should begin applauding the winning strokes of her opponents, and especially of some youngster she was erasing with ease and dispatch from the court. Meeting this sentiment for the first time, she was distressed. She was to meet it oftener as she went along.

Consequently she girded herself for the fray that afternoon with not much enthusiasm and set out to battle with anything but her customary eagerness. As she passed the referee's stand under the marquee she noticed a telegram on his desk. It was addressed to her. The referee was not there but his assistant, a thinnish young man, admitted with reluctance that the telegram was hers. She took the envelope, and turning to one side opened and read it. Then stuffing it into her pocket she picked up her armful of racquets and moved toward the entrance ready to take court. Others might show up late for matches, but not Janet. Hence she was beloved by all referees and umpires.

A few minutes later she was rallying on the court. Meanwhile the referee himself returned to his post behind that desk in the rear of the marquee. He was a short, stocky man in white flannels and a double-breasted, blue coat. There was testiness in his voice as he addressed his satellite who stood fluttering at his side.

"Where's that telegram, Allen? You didn't give it to Miss Johnson, did you?" His subordinate, with a timid air, not quite sure of himself, replied evasively.

"I . . . well . . . I didn't give it to her . . .

Mr. Roberts . . . You see she came along . . . and . . ."

The elder man's face darkened. "Can't I leave this place two minutes without something happening? First that ball trouble, and now this telegram. Do I have to leave instructions to meet every situation? I should imagine your common sense would tell you never under any circumstances to hand a player a telegram before a match. May be bad news, may upset them so they can't play; why, I remember once Bill Johnston got a wire from his wife just before he was going to play Tilden and . . ."

"I tell you I didn't hand it to her. She came along and asked for you, and I told her you were out somewhere talking to the head groundsman and would be right back. Then she saw the telegram and asked if it was for her. What could I say?"

The referee shook his head. "You ought to have known better, you ought to have known better," he mumbled.

All this time Janet was playing young Grace Butler from Miami. Janet, upset by the telegram, started badly and made several errors. The crowd in the stands imagined her opponent was forcing these errors. They applauded with considerable vigor, *lèse majesté* to which the Queen was unaccustomed. She was no longer the darling of the gallery. Dimly she appreciated this, yet although she knew it was natural enough, it annoyed her. It was like having an old friend go back on one. Before she could settle down and control herself, that long-legged infant in shorts had taken the first two games. Worse still, she saw almost for the first time that the majority of people in the stands had come down for only one reason—in hopes of seeing Janet Johnson beaten. It was a new and most uncomfortable feeling.

When the match ended she pushed hurriedly through the crowd, brushing aside a swarm of little boys and girls who demanded her autograph, shook her head at the Vice-President of Morrisons, Inc., who was trying to speak to her, and rushed off to the clubhouse. In the dressing room, hot, panting, she searched through her purse for a nickel. Or a dime. Didn't have one. One never did have one when it was necessary. Somebody changed a quarter. With trembling hands she shut herself in the steaming telephone booth. To be sure she hadn't seen much of Rodney those past weeks, but when he knew she was in trouble he would be ready to help. That was one thing about Rod. You could always depend on him, you could be sure he . . . She dialed the number awkwardly.

"Number . . . please?"

"Vanderbilt 3-2400." There was a long moment's pause. Then:

"You have *called* the wrong number. Will you please dial the number. . . . "

Impatiently she reached for the hook and got back her nickel. Now then. Again she dialed V-A-3-2-4-0-0.

In what seemed ages she heard the welcome buzzing. And a brisk woman's voice.

"Yale Club . . ."

"Mr. Rodney Davis. . . ."

Mechanically the operator repeated the name. "Mr. Davis. Hold the wire, please . . ."

Surely at six he'd be there. He was always there at six these hot days, in the pool. She knew this job of his prevented him getting down to Forest Hills much, but he always had time for exercise. While she waited, anxiously speculating, the telephone booth changed into a fireless cooker. The delay seemed eternal. Finally the operator broke in.

"Yes . . . yes . . ." said Janet, eagerly. "Hullo . . . hullo . . ."

"I'm trying to get Mr. Rodney Davis for you."

"Oh, thanks," said Janet gratefully. More waiting. Two girls, two of the players, stood outside to use the telephone next. They peered in, saw Janet, and retired discreetly across the room.

"Hullo. Are you calling Mr. Rodney Davis?"

"Yes, I am. . . ."

Another wait. It was ages. Then she came on once more. "Mr. Davis left unexpectedly this noon for the East."

"What? For where?" Janet couldn't understand, her tired brain refused to function. Rodney gone. . . . Why? . . .

"The Far East. He had to leave on several hours' notice. Are you Miss Johnson?"

Humming, throbbing in her head. "Yes," she answered.

"Miss Janet Johnson?" There it was. Always the same thing. The voice of the operator became animated. She was no longer talking to one of the dozens of feminine voices who pestered her all day long, but to a personality, a celebrity, the great Miss Johnson. The Champion. She became personal and confidential over the telephone. Her expression changed; it was the voice of a woman, not the voice of a trained telephone exchange operator. "Miss Johnson, Mr. Davis left a message for you. He said . . . he said if you called, to say he tried to get you, that he called you four times this morning at your hotel." Janet was in despair. Why had she stayed down on Long Island swimming this morning? Of all days to be away from town! "He said he tried his best to get in touch with you all over town, before his boat sailed. He said he had written you a letter . . ."

Janet stepped from the booth.

"All through, Janet?" asked one of the two girls waiting for the telephone. She went un-hearing across into the changing room without a word. The two girls watched her disappear and then looked at each other.

"Well! She's upstage, isn't she? Gets 'em all, being champion, doesn't it?"

14

Journey to Millville

With Rodney away there was only one person she could call upon: Duncan Fletcher.

But finding Duncan seemed impossible. When you wanted a person you could never get hold of them at West Side. A phone call to the referee disclosed that he was not in the marquee. A boy reported that he was not upstairs in the men's lockers. Janet began looking herself in despair. The lounge, the halls, the office, the terrace of the clubhouse. Nowhere. Finally someone volunteered the information that he had been seen fifteen minutes before in a front box in the marquee. Positively. Janet decided to take nobody's word for it, but to look for herself. Sure enough, there he was leaning on the rail watching a match.

" 'Lo, Janey." His pet expression for her. "What's up?" The somewhat disheveled condition of the usually *soignée* champion showed something wrong.

"Come on into the clubhouse. I'll tell you." He followed her as she picked her way through the crowd. "I'll tell you what's up. In just two words. My mother's seriously ill up country."

"Oh! Why, Janet . . . that's too bad. . . . What's the matter?"

"She's had an operation this morning. She was up there visiting, and this came on, and they operated suddenly. Account of the tournament she didn't want to bother me, but the doctor just wired she's critically ill."

"Phew! What you going to do?"

Janet paid no attention to this query. Instead she asked: "How much money you got on you now?"

"Money? 'Bout thirty-five dollars."

"That's no good. Now look. I'll give you my

check for two hundred. You rush over to La Guardia Field right away. Got your car here? Good."

"La Guardia Field?"

"La Guardia Field. Please do what I say. Get over there and find out how much it will cost me to charter a plane for Fairfield. I know there's a landing field at Fairfield."

"Hey, wait a minute, Janey. You aren't going up there by plane tonight, are you? You've got a tough match tomorrow."

"Listen, Dunc. Please don't argue. Get busy. At Fairfield I can find a taxi for Millville. Have the plane warmed up and ready. I've had nothing to eat since breakfast, so I'll stay and get some food after I've washed and dressed. You better phone me here at the club that it's okay, and as soon as you've phoned I'll take a taxi over to the Field. See?"

He was off. Forty minutes later as she was finishing her meal, talking to a feature writer from the Sunday *Mail*, and carrying on a conversation with the referee in an endeavor to have her next match put off until five the following afternoon, she was called to the telephone. Duncan Fletcher's voice had a disappointed tone.

"Hey, Janet. This isn't so good. The last plane for Fairfield left before I got here. There isn't another one until tomorrow morning."

Janet was furious. "Oh, Duncan, I told you distinctly to *hire* me a plane. For myself, stupid, understand? A private plane."

"*Hire* one?"

"Yes, *hire* one."

"Oh . . ."

"Oh . . . oh . . . well, what about it?"

"You mean charter a special plane to go up there tonight?"

"That's what I said."

Even though accustomed to taking orders from Janet, and extraordinary orders, too, this dazed him. "Hold on a sec." He turned to someone beside him in the office. "Well . . . Janet . . . the manager here says they won't charter a special plane unless you'll take it up and back. He says . . . he says anyhow they don't like to hit Fairfield at night because the field there isn't equipped for night landings very well. He says . . ."

"Never mind what he says. Get that plane."

"Wait a sec. What's that? Oh, Janet, he says it will be three-fifty. The check you gave me was for two hundred. Shall I give him mine for the balance? Do you want it that bad?"

Janet was now thoroughly exhausted. "Yes, of course I do. Fix it up, have the thing warmed and ready when I arrive. I'm leaving now, understand?" She rang off, and returned to the dressing room where she kept a small handbag packed and ready for emergencies. This was one the champion had never contemplated.

The machine rose into the September dusk. It skimmed over New York and on into the night. It was a small machine, but the night was clear and calm, and she watched the lights appear below. Then she heard a voice. The pilot was twiddling a radio. It was an announcer, giving a summary of the day's tennis at Forest Hills. Once again she was the champion. No one would permit her to forget it for a moment. Even at five thousand feet in the air the champion business was everlastingly with her.

In spite of herself she couldn't help listening to his glib phrases. ". . . and to recapitulate is merely to state that the favorites all came through today. . . ." What on earth was the man attempting to say? ". . . no upsets in any of the matches of the afternoon. In a grueling contest the fleet-footed Janet Johnson, our national champion . . ." Grueling indeed, thought Janet. Six–two, six–two; that's what he calls grueling. What nonsense! ". . . and besides the large gallery saw such unusualities as the defeat of Miss Dorothy Prince of San Antonio, Texas, by young Mary Lou Wilson of Los Angeles. Miss Wilson is one of the coming young Californian stars likely to make trouble . . ." Janet sat up and paid attention. Mary Lou Wilson! Yes, that was the one, a child of seventeen who even at that tender age already had a manager who had traveled East with her, winning various tournaments en route. Have to have a look at that young lady. The announcer was still talking.

". . . and on this hallowed turf, Dave Jordan, national singles champion, breezed through in his accustomed style, while Hank Stevens, second ranking player, tumbled Eric Davison, the Englishman, in yet another grueling match, six–two, one–six, six–two, six–one." Words rippled from the speaker's mouth. "By the way of interposition may I say this is the Universal Broadcasting Company bringing you a résumé of the afternoon's play at the National Singles Championships at Forest Hills . . . Long Island, an afternoon mixed with sparkling play in the men's and women's events, with several really grueling contests to thrill the large crowd in the big white stadium."

Up ahead there was a flash of lightning. The heat inside the plane was intense, and they were evidently running into a storm. Without pausing for breath the announcer continued his eloquence.

". . .Miss Jane Morrison, dainty Wightman Cupper, defeated the gazelle-like Millicent Rogers in two sets . . . while Spike Kennedy of Princeton completed the day's cannonading in a remarkably grueling battle . . . and the statuesque Betty Nickerson defeated young Grace Bennett of New York, diminutive of stature but stern of game, in two sets, six–three, six–four. So I think we've given you pretty much the entire output of the day's play . . . and here's the schedule for tomorrow . . . fleet-footed Janet Johnson goes on at five o'clock. . . ." The voice of the speaker was drowned in a clap of thunder. They were entering a storm.

Janet's mind shifted from Forest Hills to her mother. Her mother watching from a window in their home in Greenwood Heights while under the eyes of her father she whanged a tennis ball at the garage door; her mother at Cold Springs; her mother in a front box beside the court at Forest Hills; her mother waiting for her in the lobby of a New York hotel. She realized they had grown more and more apart of late years, and the fault was probably hers. Had her mother known of the immediacy of the operation and gone purposely away from Janet during the championships? It was more than likely. She was conscience-stricken as she saw how little attention she had paid her in recent months. The simple eloquence of the telegram she fingered in the pocket of her coat was terrifying.

An hour, two hours passed, most unpleasant ones for Janet who saw all at once how lonely she would be if anything happened to her mother. True, their disagreements had increased rather than decreased in recent years. But although they disagreed, they seldom fought. With her mother in danger those scenes returned to plague her. A wave of fear and loneliness came over Janet. If her mother should—if anything should happen to her, she'd be really alone. More so even than most champions. Except for Rodney. Now Rodney was disappearing from her world also.

They finally bumped to a landing, not a very good one because there was a drizzle of rain and a low ceiling. She sloshed through mud to a waiting taxi, and in a minute was off on the mountainous road to Millville. It was another hour and a half before they saw the lights of the town. The hospital was new since the days of her childhood, for the old two-story brown frame structure of her youth had been torn down and a new red brick one built on the same spot.

The matron was waiting in a reception room off the hall. Behind her a white-capped nurse was in attendance, much as the colonel of a regiment has an A.D.C. at his beck and call. She greeted the visitor with a professional air, while the young nurse stared with open eyes. Janet was drawn into the reception room at the side, a cubbyhole which had the impersonal appearance of all hospital waiting rooms with ancient magazines on a table struggling in vain to convey a homelike atmosphere.

"She's holding her own," the matron said. "That's all we can say at the moment."

"Did you get my wire?"

"Yes, Miss Johnson. We were able to move her to a private room when we received your telegram. About the specialist. Oh . . . here's

Doctor Foster now. This is Miss Janet Johnson, Doctor."

How she hated the sound of that voice rasping out her full name. Janet Johnson. Anyone else would have been Miss Johnson; she was tagged Janet Johnson for life. The little bespectacled man was new since her time. Old Doctor Browne had long since died. She saw the curious, so-this-is-the-champion look come into his face as they shook hands. His fingers were strong and competent and she began to like him. But still she hoped he had called in the specialist.

"Your mother is . . . well, I've just been up there, and she's no worse. No worse than when I wired you. That's about all I can tell you, Miss Johnson." He took off his glasses and polished them nervously. "I rather wanted . . . I was anxious tonight to call in Dr. Reynolds . . ."

"The specialist? But why didn't you?" She turned on the matron. "I specially wired you . . ."

"Yes, Miss Johnson, but you see Dr. Reynolds lives over to Fairfield and he charges twenty-five dollars for a consultation of this sort. Then of course there'd be a taxi for him up and back, because the train service is so uncertain. I didn't know . . . I wasn't quite sure . . ."

Janet addressed the doctor. "Can you get him by telephone? Right away? Good. Do so, please. Have him come immediately, by taxi if necessary. Tell him I'll be perfectly willing to spend a hundred dollars if he'll come at this hour of the night." The A.D.C. of the matron scampered across the corridor and became suddenly efficient at the switchboard. Janet could hear her.

"Fairfield 2893. This is Millville 8400. Yes . . . please . . . yes . . ."

Janet turned to the matron. "Will you find me a room and have my bag sent up? Tell the chauffeur I shan't want him again until noon . . . let's see, yes, noon tomorrow. I'd like to see my mother if it's possible. Oh, yes, and the specialist, too, as soon as he comes, please."

15

Another Title Won

It was easy enough, Janet discovered, to be on time for a match when you could arrive at the clubhouse an hour beforehand, dress slowly, and saunter forth to the court exactly when you liked. It was quite another matter after a sleepless night, when you had to taxi an hour over country roads, climb into a plane for several hours of bumpy riding over heat waves, followed by still one more taxi ride to racquet and clothes. Somehow she made it, and at five stepped breathlessly to the referee's desk to report for her match.

The contest dragged on and on. Ordinarily she would have galloped through her opponent, but she was weary, mentally as well as physically. While she was staggering to the clubhouse afterward, a thoroughly exhausted champion whose one thought was that voluptuous hot shower, the crowd was pouring from the stands saying that it only had proved what that match against that child from Florida had shown. The handwriting on the wall. Johnson's slipping. Let's see now; how old is she? And they departed discussing Mary Lou Wilson and other possible successors.

Janet had almost reached the clubhouse when she heard feet plodding on the turf behind.

"Miss Johnson! Miss Johnson!" She turned around to see Casey, the sportswriter, his forehead damp and his cheeks flushed.

"Excuse me, Miss Johnson, were you the one who hired that plane over to La Guardia Field last night?"

Janet frowned. This was something she wished heartily to keep to herself. It was something close to her, not anything connected with tennis or the business of being champion.

"Why, what are you talking about, Casey?"

The face of the squat little Irishman clouded. There they stood looking at each other. He was puzzled. "Reason I ask is, the A.P. man at the field saw you come in this afternoon and recognized you. The paper wants to know for sure; they telephoned me to check before they run the story. You see being champion makes a big difference."

The champion! Janet was in despair. Once again, and not for the last time, she felt herself enmeshed, unable to move, to perform the slightest act without attracting attention. For a minute she stood speechless, and Janet was not often without words. She saw the walls closing about her. All the while the little man remained waiting, watching and observing that the champion was tired.

At last she nodded. "Yes, Jimmy. It was— my mother's seriously ill up country and I had to see her. She's had an operation and they don't know . . ."

His admiration was so natural and so spontaneous that it did her good. That look and his tone were the only pleasant things she had seen or felt for days and weeks.

"Why, say, Miss Johnson! And you playing the championships this week! Say! There isn't many of these dames here who would risk their title like that. No, sir. Look here . . . You won't be going up again, will you?"

"I don't know yet. Not tonight anyway. What I do tomorrow depends on my mother's condition."

"The night before the finals! Mean to say you'd fly up and take chances of losing on Saturday afternoon?" This in a tone that implied, why, not even the great Janet Johnson can hope to do that and win. The great Janet Johnson admitted the justice of his tone which she understood perfectly. She could not live through another such night of strain and win the title.

"I don't know. If she needs me, I'll go. But look here, you'll keep all this out of the papers, won't you, Jim? I mean, I'd consider it a great personal favor, if you would. A favor to me. You'll speak to all the rest, to the other boys, will you, please?"

He was a trifle disturbed by the depth of the champion's feelings. Some of the boys said she was a tough customer, a pretty hard-boiled dame. But he always claimed Janet was good stuff. He always told them she was okay. Yet to see her reach the finals and then deliberately toss the title out the window, this surprised even Casey.

"Sure. I unnerstand, Miss Johnson. I unnerstand how things are. Yep, I'll tell the other boys and I'll fix things up with the city editor. Don't you worry. And say, I wish you the best of luck on Saturday afternoon."

"Thanks, Jim. I'm afraid I'll need it." He stood watching her as she went up the steps, unseeing and worried. Yes, he was afraid she would need luck, too.

As good as his word, his column carried nothing of her handicap the next morning. The trouble was that two tabloids with less fine sensibilities had gathered enough from fact and fiction to report that Miss Janet Johnson, the tennis champion, had made a midnight dash across country by airplane to the bedside of a dying relative, and that her further appearance in the championships at Forest Hills was uncertain. "At a late hour last night Miss Johnson was in her hotel here in New York, but refused to comment on the telephone."

Most of the crowd had heard about it the following afternoon, and she was greeted by an outburst of applause, a reception contrasting strongly to the perfunctory manner in which the Center Court had greeted her several days previously. But that applause was nothing to the way she was received when she came on court for the finals against Mary Lou Wilson, the one player that everyone agreed might threaten her title. It was after another exhausting trip to Millville to find her mother better although not yet out of danger. So she who never was more than a few seconds late for a match was nearly half an hour behind time that afternoon, while the referee waited impatiently, telephoning the clubhouse every three minutes to learn whether she had finally arrived.

Meanwhile Mary Lou, with Gracie Littlefield, a former amateur now turned professional, who was the girl's tennis coach, manager, and general mentor, sat dressed in her best new shorts ready to take the court. They were waiting, both somewhat nervous, the child most of all.

"I declare, I think she's done all this on purpose. Just the sort of trick she would play," remarked the elder woman in a tone that showed she was not to be taken in by any such bid for the sympathies of the gallery—sympathies which had been growing increasingly warm all week toward the young contender. The gallery sat in the stands, patient and silent, surveying the empty Center Court and reading of the latest dash of the champion to the bedside of her sick mother. As they read, they turned to each other thinking the same thought. Wouldn't it be wonderful if by any chance she did win . . . what was it . . . her fifth . . . sixth title?

Ah . . . there she is now. . . .

Tired, wan, haggard, she walked down the brick steps to the court, a different girl from the eager, alert Janet Johnson who usually faced the battalion of cameramen at the bottom with a smile. As she appeared there was a ripple of noise which grew louder and louder until it startled her—she who was so accustomed to the noise of crowds all over the world. It made her glance upward into the rows of smiling faces. Until that moment she did not realize it was for her. Her heart jumped at this outburst of affection, at this greeting from the kindly thousands above. Who indeed could withstand, who could hear unmoved that infectious, spontaneous roar, that recognition from friend to friend? She forgot the worries of the weary week behind her, forgot she was jaded and spent. With eagerness she knocked the ball across the net with a zest she had not felt for many a long afternoon.

The crowd noticed this immediately. When she won the toss and stepped to the service line, the applause surged up once more, so loud and insistent that in justice to her adversary she could not begin. In vain the umpire from his chair turned toward the crowd, appealing for silence with upraised hands. No one heeded him, nor heeded Janet bouncing the ball at her feet and waiting for the ovation to subside.

In her best new shorts, especially designed by her coach for immediate sale to a large New York department store as soon as the child had won the title from Old Lady Johnson, stood Mary Lou. Playing her first championship finals against the keenest strategist in women's tennis made her quite nervous enough. The wait added to her tenseness, and the reception for the champion increased it further. Her coach had explained all week the importance of having the gallery with you in an important match, and gleefully commented that Janet was losing it; in fact, had already lost their sympathy. The crowd wanted to see her beaten. It didn't matter, they'd be with anyone who beat her. Well, thought Mary Lou on the baseline, if Janet has lost the gallery she's getting it back rather quickly. These ideas flashed through the girl's mind as the champion stood across the court, tapping the ball. They failed to steady the youngster's shaky nerves because she realized that the reception would act as a tonic on the game of her opponent.

That was just what it did. With all her old keenness, with that marvelous sense of timing which she alone possessed, Janet leaned into a forehand straight down the line, while the crowd watched the challenger run for the corner, stab, and miss the ball by yards. The applause once again interrupted play.

"Say, who said Johnson was slipping? Some shot, that!" The commotion from above stimulated her as nothing else in the world could have done. She threw off her Nile green sweater when they changed courts after the first game. Then she went to work. Cleverly and accurately she applied pressure when pressure was necessary, used subtlety when subtlety alone would win. And at every stroke and in every rally the entranced onlookers saw further proof of the staunch heart of the girl who "would risk a title by running across three states in a plane to the sickbed of her mother . . . say, look at that backhand. . . . What a shot. . . . What a player she is!"

As Casey put it the next morning: "That most popular of all American Champions, Miss Janet Johnson of Greenwood Heights, New York, won her fifth straight title yesterday afternoon to the delight of fifteen thousand frenzied spectators, blowing young Mary Lou Wilson of Los Angeles, California, off the court. . . ."

So Casey said the following day. Casey was right, too.

16

Sir Anthony Venables, Bt.

Seven of a July morning in a suburb of London. Along one side of the street stretched a golf course, the only golf course in the world used as a parking space during a tournament of lawn tennis. Over a driveway leading onto the course from the street was a sign indicating that during the fortnight cars might be parked there for the sum of two shillings per day. Across the street from the parking space was an ugly gray, concrete structure that resembled a railway station from the outside. It was surrounded by a high, iron fence, a fence which stretched up and down the street as far as you could see. Beside this fence reaching from the wooden ticket booths at one end for almost five hundred yards was a line of people four deep, a line waiting to get cheap seats for that afternoon. The cheap seats were only put on sale at noon, and this was but a portion of the Wimbledon crowd. Many of these fanatics were sitting on camp stools, some reposing on boxes, others standing; most of them as their weary faces testified had been in line since the previous night.

Here and there a small spirit lamp blazed while its owner steeped and drank tea. Close to the line on the sidewalk moved hawkers with cushions, men with sandwiches, entertainers with banjos, comedians telling stories or singing in unpleasant Cockney tones. An occasional speculator on the fringes addressed some especially tired-looking standee with an offer of a good profit for his place in the line. At intervals were messenger boys who would remain until the persons who had hired them appeared to take their places in the line just before the gates opened at noon. Rain started to fall in the middle of the morning, a thin drizzle which discouraged none of the enthusiasts. They had arrived hours before to get an opportunity of seeing Miss Janet Johnson, and were not to be daunted by a little dampness. Instead of deserting their posts, they huddled together under umbrellas and put on raincoats, a testimony to the popularity of the champion.

Promptly at noon the gates opened. The crowd rose, folded up their camp stools and pressed slowly forward to claim their places. At this moment the champion in her suite in Dorchester House was partaking of her noonday meal. And ruminating. It was two years since her mother's death, two years of bitter struggling, of loneliness, of terrific efforts to keep ahead of the pack; of Phyllis Delacourt, the young English star; of Mary Lou Wilson, improving every month under skillful training; of others treading closer and closer on her heels.

Even the match of that afternoon against her ancient antagonist Greta Fischel troubled her; she knew the result would be in doubt until the last point. And if she won? If she won, then she would face Mary Lou tomorrow, no longer a terrified and impressionable youngster, but a schooled player with a fine game and a growing confidence in her ability, a confidence that was increasing with every match.

Never had Janet felt more lonely. She had heard from Rodney often: letters from somewhere north of Singapore in the East, but he couldn't get home. To be sure there was Tony, otherwise Sir Anthony Venables, Bt., captain in his Majesty's Life Guards.

Certainly Tony was not exciting. But he liked her, no question about that. She sighed involuntarily.

Ting-a-ling-a-ling-a-ling.

The discreet British telephone on the table at her side tinkled. "Hello. . . . Yes, tell him I'm just finishing, please. Tell him I'll be down in a minute or two." Somehow she wanted to put Tony off as long as possible. He was one of those punctual men, always on time, always ready. She longed momentarily for less punctuality and more of Rodney's impetuosity and temper. Rodney had a temper, that lad. But still . . .

Tony was waiting when she reached the lobby. He saw her step from the elevator, came forward, and shook hands as if he were thoroughly ashamed of himself for exhibiting all that sentiment in public.

"Good morning. Hope you're quite fit."

"Very well, thanks. And how did you leave the Life Guards and Windsor?"

"Oh . . . all right, I should think."

They went out together, he swinging a tightly rolled umbrella, she carrying a new racquet which had only been delivered that morning. In a white dress and a white coat with a rose on it, she was a lovely sight. No wonder people in the lobby stared as they left.

The sun was warm, the air had cleared. As they went through Kensington High Street, Janet, with that test ahead, leaned back, relaxing and enjoying the air on her face.

Soon they were coming to the rise at Wimbledon Common where R.A.C. signs pointed "WIMBLEDON." Then down the long street with hideous suburban villas half concealed behind fences and hedges, and so into the vortex of motor buses and cars converging on the stadium. As they drew near a bobby standing in the middle of the road attempted to make them turn into the golf club's parking space, but Tony slid past his outstretched arms and went on to the main entrance of the grounds. The line which had adorned the sidewalk hours before had disappeared within; only a regiment of tossed and crumpled newspapers betrayed their presence.

Another bobby stood in the center of the street. "Miss Johnson," said Tony, leaning out slightly. The magic words. The policeman moved aside, motioned peremptorily to the guards at the gate, which instantly swung apart to admit them. As it did, she noticed large boards leaning against the fence bearing the names of the afternoon newspapers, with big, red signs.

TODAY'S SEMIFINALS
JOHNSON-FISCHEL MATCH TODAY

The crowd, clustered about the entrance, moved aside and the big car entered the concrete drive-way.

The driveway was fifty yards long and led to the main entrance in the rear of the stadium. It was a wide doorway giving into the clubhouse, the offices of the Secretary, the dressing rooms, the lounge, and the Royal Box. Standing on the driveway before this entrance, with patience possessed only by the Britisher, were several hundred men and women, curiously awaiting the arrival of the star of the afternoon. In the stands these spectators were apart, distant from the performers, here they were close to them, on intimate and cozy terms. Meanwhile on the third step of the entrance was a fussy little gray-haired gentleman in a gray suit, wearing a gray necktie with pink stripes, and a worried look on his gray face as he kept glancing at his wristwatch. It was Mr. J. D. Beresford Foster, Honorary President of the All England Club which is Wimbledon. When at last he saw the gates open and the Bentley appear, his face assumed a beatific expression and he came down one step as a special concession to the importance of the newcomer. In the populace there was a craning of necks, a raising of heads while the car came to a stop before the steps; this was their great moment and they closed about the machine. A murmur of delight rose as the pretty girl in white stepped out and was greeted with a most unBritish demonstration of affection by the fussy little man in gray.

"So glad you've come a bit early, Miss Johnson," and he led the way inside. "You see . . ." He paused a moment to allow the import of his message to sink in. "You see, Her Majesty has expressed a desire to have you presented—"

"Yes, indeed," replied Janet, all her thoughts and concentration on the match ahead of her. "Afterwards, certainly." Then she stopped.

The little man's face took on a pained expression. "Ah . . . ah . . . would you very much mind . . . Miss Johnson, I know it is difficult, but would you mind very much . . ." His grief was so apparent that Janet went up the steps toward the Royal Box.

The stadium was jammed for the match and so was the Royal Box. Every eye followed her as she stepped down front preceded by the little gentleman in the gray suit. Janet carried off the moment with simple dignity. She curtsied before the Queen, shook hands, stood chatting a moment or two, curtsied again, and escaped. As she climbed the stairs and dived back into oblivion, the crowd buzzed with excitement. Of course! Janet Johnson was being presented at Court that night!

The little gray-haired man escorted her down drafty passages, up a flight of stone steps, and so to her dressing room, where he left her with expressions of gratitude. She went inside and locked the door. This was hers. The champion did not dress with the others in the main women's changing rooms below. Now she was the star of the piece and as star of the piece she had her private quarters.

With deliberation she undressed and prepared for the fray. First, and most important, her feet. Knowing that a match against a crocodile like Greta Fischel would resolve itself into a marathon, and that Wimbledon allowed no rest after the second set in which one could change clothes or repair blistered toes, she saw to it that her feet were ready. Carefully she taped the balls of each foot, and wound especially thin surgeon's plaster around her big toes, for these were the vulnerable places. This took time. Then she started to dress. First of all a pair of close-fitting, short panties, designed for a ballerina. Then a tiny brassière which she inspected minutely to be sure the hooks and eyes were securely sewed and couldn't give way. Next she took up a slip. As a rule she didn't wear a slip, hadn't for several years. But this her mother had made for her, one of the last things she had done. So Janet stepped into the slip, and took up her blue socks, blue being the color of the afternoon. Pouring foot powder into each sock, she pulled them on. More foot powder in each shoe, which she turned on end to be certain the powder got well down into the toes. Leaning over, she yanked the laces to make sure they wouldn't break, and tied them in a double knot.

Then the dress. It was the finest grade of rayon sharkskin, made by Chenard, Ltd. especially for the champion. The skirt was full, short, pleated, just to the edge of her knees.

Once a tennis dress was on, she was particular not to sit down before she went on the court, so she stood before the mirror to fix her face and hair. The champion never put on any make-up except on her lips. The blue ribbon, meticulously wound and fastened in her hair. Yes, that would do nicely. The blue belt. The tiny blue handkerchief in the pocket. There! The ensemble was satisfactory, she thought, as she surveyed herself in the smallish glass permitted the champion. Over her back she looked to see whether the slip showed behind. No, nothing. She raised her arm in a service, she went through the motions of a smash, still watching the back of her dress in the mirror. No, perfect. She was ready. Just in time.

There was a discreet knock, a mere suggestion of a knock, one might call it.

"Coming . . ." she responded. Leaning over, she unscrewed the big wooden press standing in the corner. From it she took four bats, tested the gut carefully in each, and laid them on the table. Then slipping into the delicate blue cashmere cardigan which completed her costume, she picked up the racquets with the one she had brought along that morning, and took a final look around. Had she forgotten anything? Nothing. She hated to leave. How would she feel on returning? Never yet had she come back to the little room defeated. Yet somehow she was worried; not the way, she reflected, to begin a match.

Quickly she stepped outside, closing the door behind. It was an opaque door on which were printed in largish letters the words:

THE LADY CHAMPION

Of such apparent trifles is our civilization made.

17

In the Crocodile's Jaws

Oldtimers in the stands, who had seen every match since the initial Wimbledon back on the Worple Road, said that for intensity of feeling and unconcealed hostility between the antagonists they had never seen the like of the first semi-final that afternoon.

Since their encounter years before, Janet's path had never crossed Greta Fischel's. But the German woman had not forgotten her defeat. Now she felt her moment of revenge had arrived.

Because if the American had improved in the seasons intervening, she herself was also a better player.

No one had more admiration than Janet for a person who knew his job, and from the first rally she realized this woman knew her job profoundly. That weakness on the backhand had gone with practice and tournament play. Her awkward service hardly came off the ground and needed attention to prevent errors. Even at the net the angular German with her tremendous reach had improved; she was effective if clumsy. She could volley and smash. This was serious business. Janet concentrated upon her task.

They kept even all through the set. It was a war of attrition. Apparently the German had decided to beat Janet by steadiness, no easy job, and contented herself with hitting the ball deep and keeping it in play. She had one asset, a colossal patience, as inexhaustible as her tenacity. Making no errors, she took no chances, allowing Janet these luxuries. She was willing to hit the ball a hundred times across the net to win a point, and sometimes the rallies lasted longer. Uninspiring tennis, yet, because of the two personalities involved, the gallery sat attentively watching.

At four—all, Janet decided to interject some variety into the game. With all the dexterity which she possessed she tried several drop shots in an attempt to lure the other from the base line. Unfortunately it is difficult to make a successful drop shot on balls deep in your court. Twice the German scrambled in, and with her devastating forehand put the ball away. Rounds of applause greeted her as she went ahead for the first time, five—four. This German was by no means a favorite with the gallery, but here, as at Forest Hills, the defeat of a reigning champion was a sensation.

The ninth game was everlasting. Three times Janet had a point for five—all, and each time lost it. At deuce she was blown, and double faulted. Her next service was clean, firm, down the line, and the German reached for it and hit deep to the left corner.

"Out . . ." called the linesman. Janet felt her heart thumping. By inches only, by two inches was she saved. Once again they went into an interminable rally. Will against will, each player refusing to admit the superiority of the other. Back, across, deep to the forehand, down the line, now across court again, a shot to the side which required a high lob to recover position, stretching for a slow, short one, scuttling back to position. . . .

"Games are five—all . . . first set!" Thunder broke out from the crowd. But now Janet stood exhausted, panting, her hands on her hips, weary, spent. Decidedly this was no fun, this tennis business.

She got to six—five, then seven—six, and finally eight—seven. Yet still she was miles away from the set. At ten—all she first became aware of a burning sensation in her left foot. The continual slide, slide, slide was telling. She tried to pull up her sweaty sock to relieve the pressure. No go. At twelve—all the burning sensation had become pain. There was an unpleasant feeling, too, in her other foot.

At fourteen—all she happened to glance up into the press box as she began to serve and noticed Casey, his hand over his mouth, yawning! Yes, well, tomorrow New York would read that it was a dull match. Uninteresting. To him, maybe, but not if you were out on the Centre Court struggling for your life, for your very existence. Then all at once she felt what only a great player can feel, the subconscious wavering of the will of her adversary. This punishment which was racking one was also torturing the other. After a rally Janet hit a clean forehand drive into the unprotected right corner. For the first time the German girl, instead of trying for the ball, stood watching, her mouth open in agony.

A minute later Janet heard the blessed words. "First set Miss Johnson, sixteen—fourteen." As she walked to the umpire's chair for her towel she glanced at the clock. They had been on court an hour and fifteen minutes.

The second set was close all the way through. But somehow Janet, physically spent as she was, felt easier in her mind. That marvelous machine across the net was slowly running down. Greta Fischel was good enough to stay even with her, but Janet was beating her more often in the rallies, forcing more errors, too. At five—three her foot really bothered her acutely. One more game, four points, that's about all she had left. Then it happened!

She would have sworn she tried that strap when dressing. She must have done so; she always did. It was part of the ritual of preparing for a match. But yet it had broken. The left side of her slip dragged below her skirt, and with the score fifteen—all in that ninth game Janet stopped, fumbling in her dress, and went to the umpire's chair. You can't very well play tennis when your clothes are coming down.

The umpire, who saw her reaching for the strap, leaned over and murmured something as she drew near. In her fatigue and distress over the incident she couldn't understand his remark. A hum went up round the court, for the crowd observed what had happened. The red-faced Fräulein across the net, perspiring and panting too, came toward the chair.

"It's . . . it's all right for me to run in and change, isn't it?" Janet appealed to the man above. He leaned discreetly away from his suspended microphone in order that his words should not be audible to the 17,000 spectators.

"Quite all right, I should think, Miss Johnson, provided your opponent has no objection." He looked toward the other girl who stood peering up at him, her racquet on her hips, her breast heaving.

"Pleez . . . pleez . . ."

"I say, you have no objection to Miss Johnson's changing her slip, have you? Only take a second . . ."

The German girl raised her shoulders slightly

as if to say; well, the rules are the rules. Are we playing to the rules or aren't we? She did not refuse, but she indicated plainly enough a refusal. It was true that the rules of tennis required that play should be continuous, and that nothing in the rules gave Janet the right to take time to remove her slip in the dressing room. The umpire knew the rules perfectly. He looked in dismay at Greta and then down at Janet. Nothing to be done.

"I'm so sorry, so frightfully sorry."

Janet gathered that she could default or continue as she was. With rebellion in her heart, with a feeling of intense hatred toward the German, and with the slip now drifting plainly below her skirt and hindering her movements, she went back to court.

Suppose the other strap breaks! Suppose I trip and stumble over the edge of the slip? Suppose—for the first time in years that marvelous concentration of the champion was upset. It had been a long while since she permitted emotion of any sort to interfere with the task at hand in a match of tennis. Yet try as she would, indignation choked her composure. In a few minutes games were five—all.

The gallery rustled and buzzed over the incident. They perceived exactly what had happened and they greeted the German's pull-up to five—all with silence. But Janet's disgust was too great to let her feel the gallery's sympathy. So this was tennis; this was sport; this was a game!

Yet her competitive spirit kept the champion in the game. Despite the handicap of that broken garment, despite her ruined feet, despite the disturbance to her concentration, she managed to stay even. Her feet pained more and more, the slip fell lower and lower, but as she gradually got control of herself at six—all she began to hit again. By this time spasms of burning pain were shooting up her legs. Another thirty-game set was out of the question. She'd have to win and win quickly or else default.

So with all she had, Janet attacked. Attacking meant exchanging twenty or thirty shots before she got the one right ball to hit. Then it meant cracking a lob, another lob, and another with her whole frame aching. It meant playing on nothing but nerve. She was seven—six, she was forty—fifteen. Victory. Victory at last. Only one more point, one little point. Then twice the German, at a point from defeat, passed her with clean, low drives, and even the hostile gallery could not help showing its admiration.

Janet reached her third match point. Endlessly she fenced from the baseline, waiting like a cat for the ball to clout. Here it was! She came into forecourt. A volley. Another which pulled her out to one side. She dashed across the net back into place, and with outstretched racquet caught a passing shot and volleyed it to the corner. Hours, ages went by before the idiot on the line moved. Then he rose. The ball was good.

The German tossed her racquet to the ground beside the umpire's chair and turned her back on the victor. Janet was delighted. She had resolved that if she won she wouldn't shake hands with her opponent. Leaving that lady sucking half a lemon and sputtering harsh Teutonic syllables to a compatriot in the front row of the stands behind the chair, Janet dropped her racquets on the bench, and with her slip now well wrapped about her knee hobbled in toward the refuge of the dressing room. There, standing exactly as he had stood years before, was Rodney.

"Oh . . . Rod!" She literally tumbled into his arms, and as she did so burst into tears. Not since her mother's death had Janet shed tears, and only once after a match—her first finals at

Forest Hills when she had been badly defeated, years and years before.

"Rodney . . . Rodney . . ." she sobbed. "Please . . . take me . . . away . . . from all this . . ."

"You bet, honey, you bet. That's just what I came for."

Ordinarily it took Janet a long while to change after a hard match. She enjoyed her hot bath—no showers at Wimbledon. But Rodney was waiting. Repairing her bleeding and swollen feet as best she could, Janet dressed hastily and went down to meet him. They rushed out to the gate and climbed aboard the first taxi in the line.

"Dorchester House," she said.

"Yes, Miss." The chauffeur started his ancient vehicle, observing that his passenger was clinging to the arm of the tall man inside.

"Oh, Rodney! I'm so glad you've come at last." Then suddenly Janet sat up straight and burst out laughing.

"My goodness! I completely forgot."

"What? Who?"

"Tony Venables. He's waiting at the other entrance to take me back to the hotel."

18

The Champion Makes a Decision

The waiter knocked at the door of Number 452, the suite of Miss Janet Johnson, the tennis champion. A man opened the door and for just a second the waiter wondered whether he had the right room. That suite was Janet's castle where she was alone from the world, and in the years he had served Miss Johnson the waiter had seen few visitors and almost no men there.

"Come in, Oldham," said the voice of the

champion from the drawing room inside. She was sitting with her shoes off and her martyred feet upon a cushion placed on an Empire chair. Another Empire chair was drawn up close to hers. The waiter set the tray on a small table beside the three chairs, and, looking round to be sure everything was there, retreated.

"Shall I pour for you?" asked Rodney.

Janet sighed happily. She was in the condition when even pouring a cup of tea was a real effort. What a nice idea! "Yes, please do."

"Strong. Milk. No sugar. Unless you've changed your habits, which by the look of your figure you haven't."

Imagine him remembering that! Imagine anyone remembering. She stirred her tea and took the toast he offered. Then she drank slowly. Heavenly, health-giving nectar! Soon she felt somewhat revived. He sat down close to her big chair, hitching his nearer. He was older, his face was tanned and slightly lined, but every once in a while she observed the naughty boy of Marchmont. There was a delicious intimacy in having him here, right in the room with her, the room which saw no male save the occasional but impersonal Oldham and the even more occasional Mr. Whitley, the Managing Director. His hat and raincoat were slung over the back of one of the Empire chairs, making the room still more personal and adding further intimacy to the general situation. How wonderful it was to have him again. Of all persons on earth he was the one she most desired with her at that moment. She hadn't been looked after like this since the death of her mother. He was a buffer between her and the world, that terrible world in which but a few hours previously she had only had two choices.

". . . so that's the whole story." He offered her more toast. "Go on . . . eat it, you need something. Yes, that's the reason I never came before. Until they shoved me into this job."

"My dear, you came just in time. Just in time. Yes . . . more tea, please. You know, Rod, I never realized until you loomed up in the doorway how much I needed you."

"Well, honey, that's what I'm here for. But I was lucky to get here just the same. Tight work on the New York end. You see being in the East puts you out of touch with things like tennis, sort of. I mean I followed you almost every month when the papers from home came in, but I didn't remember July meant Wimbledon and London for you. Believe me, it took some wangling to make them let me go back this way."

"Why? Why do they care when you return? Haven't you leave of any sort?"

"Ordinarily, yes. But not these days. They want me back as soon as possible because things are so unsettled in the East. There's no one to run the show; my assistant died and the new man is a young Englishman who's only been out a few months. Then coming here to London instead of sailing direct from San Francisco means a delay of several weeks. But I stood up to the boss. I stuck to it. I said I'd go back this way or resign." He looked at Janet in the chair, thinking how lucky it was he'd insisted.

If he hadn't been stubborn, if he hadn't held out in the face of pressure, they would have pushed him back as soon as possible. "They" meant Morris, the vice-president in charge of overseas sales, and the main office in New York. What did they care about Janet? Well, he stuck to it. He'd won out. Now he had won her, won her forever, someone he loved who loved him. It was too wonderful to be true. To think he'd come at the one particular moment when she was nearing the breaking point. He didn't need to know her as well as he did to appreciate how difficult life had become. No wonder, he thought, for he could realize the strain that was continuous on the champion.

"You see . . ." he continued, "things have been terribly upset the last year in the F.M.S."

"F.M.S.?"

"Where you're going, honey. The Federated Malay States, your home, your future home, Mrs. Davis."

Mrs. Davis! Janet threw back her arms in relief. No more Janet Johnson. No more champion business. No more struggles to stay on top. No more agonies like those of the afternoon during which she had lived a thousand years and died a thousand terrible deaths. Tomorrow, win or lose—and now she was confident of victory —the champion was through. She was finished with it all, away from tennis forever, away from the Greta Fischels and Gracie Littlefields and all the rest of the tribe. These players all had homes, mothers, families, distinct and apart from the courts. But once plunged into the circuit, tennis became their life. Their backgrounds clashed with the background of the sport; homes, mothers, families, faded away. Their talk, their thoughts, their energies, hopes, and fears were bound up in one thing: the game for which they existed. From June to October tennis was their religion, their world, their everything. Well, it was hers no longer. Now that she was escaping she was able for the first time to see the whole sorry business as it really was.

"Tonight . . . ?" He was asking a question. "Oh, Rod . . . tonight I can't . . ."

"But can't we eat together our first night in two years?" His eagerness touched her. "The first time since . . . since . . ."

She grasped his hand. "My sweet, it's impossible. Don't put on that worried look of yours. It won't get you anything. I'd rather be with you this evening than anyone else in the world. This thing was arranged weeks and weeks ago. You see I'm being presented, Rodney."

"Presented?"

"Uhuh. Presented at Court. He's coming to dress me in . . . in an hour."

"To dress you!"

"Yes, young Eric Handley who designed the dress. It's a tremendous affair, getting into the dress and the feathers in your hair and all that rot. I know . . ." she threw up her arms in weariness. "I know what you think. It's absurd. So do I . . . now. Yes, the whole thing's all too silly for words. But this was arranged weeks and weeks ago. Remember until the end of that match today I hadn't any idea you were on this side of the world."

"Of course. I understand, Janet. Well, as a matter of fact the boat train got into Waterloo at two-twenty and I was at Wimbledon at ten past three. Not so bad, is it? Twelve—all in the first set when I came in; none too happy you looked, either."

She passed her hand over her eyes. That torture didn't bear thinking about. "Don't . . . I was forgetting it. That dreadful, dreadful creature."

"Well, look here, if you'll be busy all this evening . . ."

"I'm afraid I will, dear. The car calls for me with Mrs. Garrettson at seven when I'm supposed to be dressed. I shan't be back until eleven-thirty or twelve because it will be at least nine-thirty before we get into the Palace. And you can imagine how I'll feel at midnight!"

"Naturally. Poor girl! You'll be absolutely

beaten. Hadn't we better plan then, right now, about tomorrow? Your packing and all that?"

"Oh . . . the hotel maid will do that for me. I've a million and one things to settle, but I suppose they can be arranged in the morning. It's lucky I've got almost everything I own right here in this suite. What time does . . . do we leave?"

"Victoria, four-thirty. The P. & O. Boat Train."

"Four-thirty!" There was sudden alarm in her tone. She sat up. "But, darling . . . I won't be through the match by then."

"Oh! But you must be."

"But, Rod, how can I be? We go on after the finals of the mixed, that'll be two-thirty, that means . . . three-thirty . . . quarter to four at the earliest."

"Well, Janet, I *must* make that boat. Got to make it. They're already worried about my going back this way; it takes so much longer."

"But, Rodney, a day or two, the next boat, next week . . ." There was appeal in her voice, in her eyes, in the way she touched his arm.

"The next boat leaves in ten days. Anything can happen out there in ten days; suppose something did and I wasn't on hand; how'd I feel?

Point is, this one tomorrow touches at Singapore, the other doesn't go beyond Bombay." He waited anxiously, but she sat there saying nothing. "Come along, dear. You will come, you *must* come, you've *got* to come."

"Rodney, Rodney, how can I? That finals against that girl . . ."

"Why on earth not?"

"Why not?"

"That's what I said."

"You mean default?" She was shocked, the champion was shocked. To tell the truth she was not as much shocked as she pretended to be; the idea had been fluttering in the back of her mind, had penetrated a tiny bit. "Oh, I couldn't. I never did . . ."

"Well, Helen Moody did. You've got a better reason. Or haven't you?"

She couldn't resist smiling at this ingenuous appeal. It was so terribly convincing. Rodney felt himself winning. He leaned toward her. "Look, I've waited two long years until I had a decent job and could offer you a home. I've fought with my boss, risked my position, traveled across an ocean, all for you. Come along, dear, come along and let me show you all the wonderful spots of the world: Port Said by moonlight, and those hours of magical steaming through the Canal with the desert on each side, and Basra on the Persian Gulf where the villas are white with red roofs against the bluest of blue skies, and Penang, the most lovely place of all. . . ."

"But, Rod, dear, don't you see, don't you appreciate that I cannot possibly leave tomorrow like that? Just sort of drop out as you suggest . . ."

"You mean to say you don't want to come."

"Now you're being childish. Of course I want to come. I love you and I want to be with you . . ."

"All right, then come along."

"But this match . . . this finals . . . my last . . . I'm the champion, how can I quit?"

"Quit! Quit. Ha! That's a hot one. Surely this isn't quitting, you of all people. Why, you've beaten the girl a half a dozen times. You aren't afraid of her; you've given about one thousand proofs in the past ten years you aren't a quitter. *You* talk about quitting! With feet like that? Once we used to martyr ourselves for an ideal; now we kill ourselves for a challenge cup."

He was making Janet actually ashamed of her feet. She withdrew them hastily from the chair.

They immediately sent up a reminder in the shape of an angry twinge in her leg. "Oh, I couldn't really . . . what would people think?" Yet to herself, facing the problem, she realized she didn't care what people thought, that she might default, that she could, that she probably would . . . Then he said the one thing to upset her. It wouldn't have upset her had she been herself. She was a weary and beaten girl.

"You love me. You'll marry me. You'll follow me to the East. You know I've loved you . . . ever since . . . well, you know how long. Yet now . . . here you say . . . you won't . . . Oh, well, remember what I always told you. Remember I always said if you didn't look out you'd stop being a woman some day and become just a champion."

It was the last straw. Her nerves, as lacerated as her body, rebelled. That was Rodney all over. That was his point of view. Men were all alike, all, every one. Rod was terribly unreasonable. He was so stubborn. He only saw things from his angle. He was—yes, she loved him, but he was pig-headed. And at the moment she didn't love him a bit.

"I do wish you wouldn't bring that up."

"But see here. You say you love me. You want to marry me." He was dead serious now and she couldn't help noticing that his forehead was damp and his hair matted down on his brow.

"I do."

"Yet you won't give up that match when I explain it's absolutely necessary."

"No, I will not."

There! It was out. She hadn't meant to say it. Five minutes, three minutes before she was ready to yield, to give up the whole thing, but his stupidity roused her fading determination. After all, she had her life to complete, she couldn't toss everything away at a moment's notice. Why should she?

He stood, looking down at her defiantly.

"All right. If you don't love me enough . . ."

"Please don't say that." She wanted to cry again, to fall into his arms. If only he hadn't been so aggravating, so unreasonable.

"For the last time. Will you come to Singapore tomorrow and marry me?"

"No!" The champion was speaking. Yet it took all the willpower of the champion to get the word out.

"Good-bye then." He picked up his hat and overcoat. She wanted to call, to shout, to cry to him to return. Some men might relent, some men might call her on the telephone the next day; not Rodney. Then he was moving toward the door, the stupid, conceited, stubborn idiot. Let him go. The door shut. He couldn't have heard the champion say:

"Good-bye."

19

Janet Almost Changes
Her Mind

The Landaulette moved up Constitution Hill toward Hyde Park Corner. Through a haze of weariness Janet remembered the crowds outside the Palace, the lights, the music . . .

"Well, thank heaven, that's over," said Mrs. Garrettson.

"Yes." Her voice was tired. "That's over."

"You can drop me at the corner; I'll get a taxi . . ."

"How absurd! We'll take you home."

"In that case you get out at Dorchester House and have him take me on to my hotel. You need the rest, you look tired."

Janet was too weary to argue. "Dorchester House, Perkins." The Daimler slid with the traffic into Park Lane and slithered to a stop before the hotel, where a man in uniform at the entrance opened the door and helped her alight. She walked rather unsteadily across the lobby to the elevators. In a minute she was pushing the button in her own suite and sinking into the blissful comfort of the armchair. From where she sat she could see Rodney leaving the room, his brow damp, his face set, so stubborn, so pig-headed. What a man! If only he weren't quite so unreasonable. A feeling of righteousness took possession of her, yet she was not so sure about her righteousness. She felt somewhat less righteous than earlier in the evening. After all, one thing was true: she had won dozens of titles. What difference did another make?

There was a knock. "Come in. Here I am, Marie. Yes, it went very well, very well indeed. The Queen? Uhuh, she was lovely. Now get me out of this harness."

The maid began to unhook, unstrap, and unfasten the creation of Mr. Handley. She was by no means as reverent in her gestures as she had been beforehand. Janet resolved the problem in her mind. Yes, maybe Rodney had something to be said for his viewpoint after all. Of course he was stubborn, he was the most stubborn of men. But that was one of the defects of his good qualities. You had to take people as you found them. Janet found herself becoming philosophical. It was true that he was stubborn, but every great athlete is stubborn; he has to be to win. If he doesn't win he isn't a great athlete. And there you are.

Only being a man, Rodney was silly at times. Well, she'd have to think the whole question over; consider it from all sides carefully. Now that she was alone she could see things more clearly and also more dispassionately. Maybe it really *was* foolish to play. Any physician who got one look at her feet would order her to bed, or at least order her not to play in the finals on any account. She had a valid reason for defaulting with those bleeding feet. Nor could people say she had done an injustice to the girls she'd beaten, because her feet had only just gone back on her. Why shouldn't she default? Rodney was right, too, when he said no one would believe she was afraid.

She slipped on a dressing gown and, taking one from the pile of evening newspapers which were sent up every night, sank again into the armchair. It was the *Standard*. On the front page was a box enclosing the words:

"JANET CAN'T WIN SAYS MARY LOU'S COACH."

Oh! Can't I really? Instantly her spine stiffened. She became the competitor again, and folding the newspaper with a vicious smack she went on reading, while the maid fluttered between the drawing room and the bedroom disposing of the regalia of the evening. Janet ran her eye up and down the column. The article had evidently been written by Grace Littlefield, Mary Lou's coach, after the match against Greta Fischel.

"We gave Janet Johnson's old-fashioned baseline game back to the Indians long ago. She won't get a set from Mary Lou Wilson tomorrow."

The champion flushed. She was a philosopher no longer. This thrust hit home. Never a consistent volleyer from her junior days, Janet realized as she grew older she was volleying less and less. The match against the German had been waged almost entirely from backcourt until the final game. The fact that the thrust contained some truth hurt. She got red and hot; tears came to her eyes as she tried to read.

"Next season everyone will be beating Janet. The parade has passed her by. The girls aren't afraid of her any more, so I'm sticking my neck out here and now. Mary Lou Wilson will volley her right off the Centre Court tomorrow. She'll pin her ears back so hard the champion won't win three games a set."

Janet threw the paper to the ground and stood. The parade had passed her by. Had it really! Her baseline game was old-fashioned. Ha! She'd see about that. Nervously she dabbed at her eyes, walked up and down the room; no longer thinking of her aching feet, no more a woman in love, no longer faced with any decision. The decision was made. She was not a philosopher, she was a champion, and her steps quickened. Back and forth, back and forth. She realized the maid was talking. What was it?

"Yes, that's all, Marie."

"Good night, Miss."

"Good night."

So. She was through. They'd given her old-fashioned game back to the Indians. Leaning over she picked up the newspaper, reread the paragraph. Faster she moved across the room, her weariness vanishing, her feet forgotten, ready and anxious to take court against that long-legged girl in shorts. Won't get a set! Won't I, though! We'll see about that. She started planning her campaign and as she did so her anger subsided. So perfect was her control that again she became the cool, resourceful champion. Her lips were set, she had already stepped upon the packed Centre Court before those cheering thousands, ready for battle . . .

20

Finish of a Champion

It began, continued, and ended on a different note from any match she had ever played. Taking the girl's first service she smacked it down the line and came to the net. Mary Lou was so surprised she returned an easy shot which Janet volleyed away for the point.

The umpire called "Love–fifteen," the crowd leaned forward applauding, and the server shook her blonde mane in annoyance and imperiously called for another ball.

To have a carefully prepared plan of battle is one thing, but it's vastly harder to put that plan into execution if your adversary won't permit. Mary Lou and her coach had studied Janet's game with attention all through the fortnight. They had watched that endless baseline duel of the semi-finals from the front row of the players' section of the stands, with paper pads on their laps and pencils in their hands. At the hotel they had studied and analyzed those notes. From them the way to beat the champion was fairly plain. Any good volleyer could defeat Janet with ease. Mary Lou was tall, a superb volleyer, a player of quick reflexes, young, active, strong, and devastating overhead. Furthermore she had the forcing shot on her forehand behind which her volleying coups could be launched. Their confidence grew as they came up to the finals. It was in the bag!

But to the girl's surprise that afternoon the champion was not the same Janet Johnson. She was keener, there was a sting in her ground shots, and she refused to remain obligingly on the baseline. Instead of playing a passive game she grabbed the offensive herself, kept boring into the net—a place she had no business to be—at every chance. Mary Lou hit harder than the German but she lacked the Fräulein's ball control, and invariably in the rallies Janet had a shot she could smack. How she smacked it!

Bang, to the left corner. Bang, to the right. Across court, down the line swept the famous Johnson forehand, more severe and deadly than ever. It bombarded the youngster's court, and often the reply was easy to volley. Almost invariably, too, Janet was on top of the net waiting to put the reply away. Between rallies the champion limped slightly, and once or twice she winced as she ran for a shot, but when the ball was in play she was lightning on the court. Now she was enjoying herself; she played this game as she hadn't since the old days when she first appeared in championship tennis. Occasionally she was cleanly passed but she was tennis-wise enough not to permit this to worry her or change her tactics. Still she pushed into the net. Annoying stop volleys caught the challenger anchored behind the baseline. Janet's smashes were seldom severe but so angled that they were more often point winners than not.

Mary Lou tried coming in behind her high-bounding service. The Johnson forehand cut past like an express train. She served to the left court and was beaten by that backhand dragged sharply across the net. Then in one of the rallies she struck her forehand hard and came in. Janet fairly leaped at the ball. There was vehemence in her return. It came at the girl so fast she was thrown momentarily back on her heels. Stunned, she managed to get her bat to the ball and volley it. Janet cracked the return past her before she could recover balance. The applause continued so long that both players stood with heaving breast, their backs to the court, waiting for the noise to subside.

"There! How'd you like that? I'm still champion . . . young lady . . . understand . . . Still champion. . . ." Throwing the ball to serve, she caught it with all the strength of her shoulder and hips, sending it to the far corner of Mary Lou's sideline.

"Game, Miss Johnson. Games are three—love . . . first set . . ." You would have thought she was English and their own. The Wimbledon galleries, ever loyal to old favorites, cheered. "What a game! And what a player Johnson is! Still the best of the lot, isn't she?"

Mary Lou was rocked; who wouldn't be? But

she was a fine player, she could not otherwise reach the finals at Wimbledon. She wavered before the storm, but she did not crack. Her plan of battle was ruined for the moment, her expression was one of annoyance as she was beaten time and again by stop volleys or outguessed in the exchanges inside the service line. Vexed, flushed, disturbed; yet her control never weakened. The score might be one-sided, but every game was a battle in itself.

At four—love Janet caught her breath for a second. Instantly the youngster showed the stuff of which she was made by jumping to the attack. She still had command of herself and her game. With two manlike smashes she put away the champion's best lobs and won the game. Janet realized she could not relax a second. They changed courts and again the champion became a tiger as she surged into forecourt for the kill. Bang. There! Bang! So . . . you've given . . . Johnson's baseline game to the Indians . . . have you? Bang. Bang. A smash. A volley into uncovered territory.

The crowd shrieked and yelled its approval while the long-legged youngster stood biting her lips and hitching nervously at her shorts. Janet was a killer now, remorseless and without pity, out to win quickly, cruelly if need be. She got a glimpse of Casey in the press box, leaning forward, his face aglow. What a story!

Her concentrated determination stayed with her. Bang! Another drive across court. Bang to the opposite corner! Five games to one. Then in the next game she cracked the child's service with terrific speed to the baseline and made three winning volleys Mary Lou could not reach. The crowd stood applauding, a tribute to her courage and her game. Wimbledon had never seen the champion like that, had never seen such tennis before.

The two girls were standing by the net wiping their hands and faces. Janet was grim. She was thinking; won't get a set from Mary Lou Wilson tomorrow . . . Mary Lou will pin her ears back so hard . . .

There was no answer to such playing. Grace Littlefield twisted uncomfortably in her seat, wishing, as the tempest showed no signs of abating, that she had been less dogmatic in print. The slaughter on the court continued. If Janet was tiring, she gave no outward signs.

Tiring? No, she was still fresh and keen. Because every volley was solace, every game was balm to the champion. She could have gone on forever. They changed courts after the first game of the second set, and Janet walked briskly toward the baseline. Then her eye caught the clock in the corner beside the Royal Box. Three-thirty.

Victoria, four-thirty!

That clock brought her back to the real world. Something happened within her. In an hour, sixty short minutes, he'd be gone. He was going now, right now. What on earth was she doing here before this crowd, satisfying her vanity, taking revenge on a brainless child? And all the time he was going away, going out of her existence. She was a fool, she was insane! For the sake of her pride, that was it, just for her pride she was allowing him to vanish into the East. Why, she didn't even have his address! Panic overcame her. What stupidity! This tennis, this match, what would it matter in ten years. When he was going, leaving her right now . . .

"Games are two—love, Miss Johnson leads, second set, first set Miss Johnson, six games to one. Miss Johnson serving." Miss Johnson never served again.

She walked in to the umpire's chair while a

peculiar kind of hush fell over the watching crowd. "I'm defaulting." The umpire gasped. He'd heard, yet he hadn't understood. Mary Lou, seeing something was happening, came toward the net. Janet turned and in a low voice said:

"You're champion. Congratulations! I'm off . . . I'm defaulting." Picking up her racquets she rushed from the court, past the linesmen sitting with open mouths, past astonished officials standing in the entrance ready to congratulate her as the winner, and so up two steps at a time to her own quarters. Taylor, the attendant, was picking up the room.

"Taylor! Quick! Pack all my bags. Yes, all three, the suitcase . . . my street clothes . . . and have Perkins come up for them at once. . . ." She turned to the telephone.

"Grosvenor 4800. Please. . . . Get on with it, Taylor; don't stand there gaping . . ."

"Yes, Miss; yes, Miss Johnson." The champion must be out of her head!

"Dorchester?" She was panting. "Give me . . . the Managing Director . . . please . . ." There was a wait during which she began to feel her feet throbbing and burning. Finally his secretary responded.

"The Managing Director? I'm rather afraid Mr. Whitley's busy just now."

"Miss Beckford! This is Janet Johnson."

"Oh, Miss Johnson." There was a noticeable change in her tone. "He's with the Chairman of the Board. I'll see if I can put him on to you." A longish pause. Then the polished voice of the Managing Director. Wonderful example of the power of the Wimbledon champion as against the power of the Chairman of the Board of the Gordon Hotels, Ltd.

"Congratulations, Miss Johnson!" He had evidently heard the first set over his wireless and assumed she had finished and won. She cut him short; no time for small talk.

"Mr. Whitley. I'm in great trouble. Can you . . . will you help me out?"

"Of course, Miss Johnson. Anything at all, a pleasure . . ."

"Have Marie, the maid on the fourth floor, pack my bags . . . yes, everything in the suite, immediately. Everything. Then send them with your most reliable courier down to the P. & O. boat train. Victoria . . . four-thirty."

"But . . . Miss Johnson . . . it's three thirty-five . . . three-forty almost, now."

"I know. But I'll be there . . . I'll be at the train gate . . . and Mr. Whitley . . ."

"Yes, Miss Johnson . . ."

"Would you cash a check for twenty pounds? I'll give the Dorchester man the check . . ."

"Certainly, Miss Johnson. With great pleasure."

"And Mr. Whitley. My bill." Although her expenses were paid by the United States Tennis Association, sundry extras, usually amounting to a considerable sum in the six weeks' stay, were paid by Janet herself.

"Miss Johnson!" The Managing Director became distressed. There was anguish in his tone. "We'll forward it to you, wherever you are."

"No, I'm going out to the East. Suppose you have the bill brought down to the train and I'll send up a check from Marseilles. Is that clear?"

"Quite, Miss Johnson. I shall attend to the matter myself." His tone showed no surprise whatever. Apparently no vagary of human nature could astonish or upset the urbane Managing Director. She rang off as Perkins, cap in hand, arrived for the first bag that Taylor had just shut and locked.

21

Start of a Long Journey

Y ou can make it, Perkins. You can make it,
can't you?"

The huge Daimler hummed smoothly up the
rise past the golf club, overtook a bus, and
skimmed into the straight road by Southfields
Underground Station. Without turning his head
or relaxing his grip on the wheel, he said:

"Do my best, Miss. Depends on the traffic in
the city. Isn't much time, you know!" A clock
in the square showed twelve to four. Victoria;
four-thirty!

"Oh, you must, Perkins, you must." She compared her wristwatch with another clock. Hers was fast, it was always fast, three minutes fast. Three minutes; one hundred and eighty seconds, that might mean the difference between . . . between . . . Oh . . .

Perkins dextrously swerved as a truck without warning came into the middle of the road. He cut back just in time to avoid an oncoming taxi, and shot ahead down a long street with which she was unfamiliar. It was a new approach, quicker, she hoped. A clock on a pub when they were stopped by a traffic light showed six minutes to four. Oh, get me there in time! Let me catch that train! Victoria; four-thirty.

They inched forward, now in the usual traffic jam at Putney Bridge. She counted the precious seconds: thirty, forty, fifty. Then again a slow movement ahead and once more a wait. She must do something; anything at all. Fumbling with her bags she determined to change her tennis shoes. At least she could change her shoes and stockings. Just in time she realized how ridiculous that was. Bad enough to appear on the platform of the boat train in tennis clothes; but to appear in tennis clothes and patent leather shoes with heels would be even more absurd.

There! At last! They were over the bridge. Another delay ahead. The seconds clicked by and every one was sheer torture. Finally they moved. Perkins turned to the right, slid into a back street lined with rows of ugly little houses on each side. Then another turn into another mean back street, his horn beating a most un-British tattoo. Victoria; four-thirty.

He certainly knew London, Perkins did. If anyone could do it, he could. "Kings Road, Kensington, S.W.," said a street sign. She looked at her watch. Eight minutes past! Oh, Rodney; I'm coming, I'm coming, Rodney, as fast as Perkins and the Daimler can make it.

They slurred past an intersection, round one of London's squares, a green oasis in the center. Dear God, please let me catch that train. Never had the champion wanted anything so much in all her life.

"You'll get me there in time, won't you, Perkins, you'll get there . . ."

"Do my best, Miss. What time is it?"

"Twelve . . . almost thirteen." Almost thirteen! Each second counted now. The chauffeur, every bit of him directed to the wheel, was noncommittal.

"H'm . . . touch and go, Miss Johnson."

There ahead was another square. A sign on a cross street read: "Chelsea, S. W." Not far now. But here the traffic grew heavier and progress was slow. No darting in and out of the line but an aggravatingly tedious crawl. Fifteen, sixteen, almost twenty past. Ahead was Sloane Square. She knew where she was now. In a minute they were riding through the leafy park in the middle of Eaton Square, and she made out the Grosvenor Hotel up ahead. Journey's end.

But that final last block of traffic snarled up around Grosvenor Gardens impeded their progress, and the clock over the Continental entrance to Victoria Station showed four twenty-three as the car came to a stop, and Janet jumped out followed by Perkins, her racquets under his arm and a small bag in each hand. They rushed through the ticket office. No time for tickets. The clock was four twenty-five. Then onto the platform.

There at the train gate was no courier but the groomed figure of Mr. Whitley himself. Over the train gate at his head were the welcome words on a large sign: "P. & O. BOAT TRAIN. VICEROY OF INDIA EXPRESS. MARSEILLES PORT SAID BOMBAY."

Mr. Whitley handed her a large manila envelope. "Money. Your passport which we took from your bag. The bill. I think you'll find everything in order." What a man! Yes, he had certainly attended to things. It was all there. "Quick, now, porter . . ." He summoned a porter who was standing at one side with Janet's luggage on a small truck. A good friend, that's what he was. Her heart leaped and sang.

"Tickets, please." A guard at the train gate stopped them.

"This lady hadn't time for a ticket. She's catching the Viceroy at Marseilles."

The guard was British; therefore he was polite, but he was also firm. "Sorry, sir." He held his hand across the entrance. "Sorry, this is a Pullman. All seats must be booked in advance. We can't allow anyone in without a ticket."

Her heart ceased to leap. The song died away. Good heavens! The fool wouldn't really stop her. He couldn't ruin it all now, when she was here, with Rodney right beyond that barrier, on the platform just a few yards away. Precious seconds ticked. But the Managing Director of the Dorchester, being English, refused to become ruffled. He turned, walked across the platform to a little man in a blue uniform, opened his purse, and she saw a ten-shilling note and his calling card change hands. The little man who had COOKS on the band of his cap drew himself up and saluted Mr. Whitley. He galvanized into action at once, coming over to the train gate and holding an earnest colloquy with the guard. The guard shook his head. He remained adamantly British and uncorruptible. While the clock on the platform above ticked out Janet's life blood.

There they stood, Janet, Mr. Whitley, Perkins with the bags, and the porter with the rest of her stuff on the truck, all waiting. The Southern Railway, in the person of the guard at the gate, continued stern and immovable. Black despair settled over Janet.

Then an official of some sort, also in railway blue, who was watching at the side, leaned over the barrier.

"Beg pardon, Miss . . . Aren't you Miss Janet Johnson, the tennis champion?" For the last time in her life she was to hear that phrase and for the first time it sounded heavenly in her ears.

"Oh . . . yes, I am. . . . I was trying . . . I simply must get the Boat Train . . . could you help . . ."

"Right this way, please, Miss." He stepped

round the barrier to her side. "Your luggage?" He led the procession, Janet at his side, Mr. Whitley just behind, followed by Perkins and the porter with the truck. In order not to defy his subordinate and thus ruin discipline on the Southern Railway, they circled back through the luggage room where with furious last-minute gestures trunks were being weighed and trundled to the train. Oh, wonderful, oh, exquisite Britain! Wonderful, exquisite man! He was talking to her, but for once the control of the champion had vanished and she was so excited she could hardly understand his words.

"Yes, my missis likes to watch you play . . . yes, indeed . . . plays quite a nice game herself, the missis does!" Janet thanked heaven that she was still in tennis clothes, that she hadn't stopped to change. Oh, blessed, oh, darling man. He continued talking as they walked onto the platform of the sacred train. "Yes, Miss, she was at Wimbledon this afternoon . . . by the way, how'd you manage, Miss? The finals today, wasn't it? Did you come out all right?"

They were going down the platform now. Sleek, blue Pullmans with signs on the sides of each car. "P. & O. BOAT TRAIN. VICEROY OF INDIA

EXPRESS. MARSEILLES PORT SAID BOMBAY."
Somewhere in one of those cars . . . her eyes
ranged the interiors.

"Oh, yes . . . I came out all right." Thanks
to him, she *had* come out all right.

•

On the platform stood the passengers of the
Viceroy of India. They were the Empire-build-
ers, the elect of the earth, tall, well-groomed
men and women as sleek and polished as well-
kept racehorses. Children attended by Indian
ayahs looked from the windows of the Pullmans.
The final farewells had been exchanged, the last
piles of luggage, the last bags of golf clubs stowed
aboard, the ultimate dilatory passenger had
clambered up the steps, when a queer group
rushed hurriedly down the platform. Everyone
on the train turned to watch them.

In front with a railway superintendent was a
flushed girl in tennis costume. She wore a red
ribbon in her hair, a red belt round her waist,
and red socks over her ankles. There was a faint
whistle, a sort of "peep-peep" from the distant
head of the train. The girl suddenly stopped,
shouted something, and jumped into a compartment. On the platform they were shoving her

stuff through the swinging door as the train gently and silently left the station behind.

Within the Pullman passengers lounging in their seats watched the drama on the platform. They saw the strange procession arrive, heard the whistle, and observed the girl jump unceremoniously into the compartment. Someone leaned across the aisle to his neighbor.

"Look here, that girl in the next car kissing that tanned man, the girl all in white tennis clothes . . . yes . . . isn't that Janet Johnson, the tennis champion?"

Turn the page to discover more exciting books in the Odyssey series.

Other books in the Odyssey series:

William O. Steele
- ☐ THE BUFFALO KNIFE
- ☐ FLAMING ARROWS
- ☐ THE PERILOUS ROAD
- ☐ WINTER DANGER

Edward Eager
- ☐ HALF MAGIC
- ☐ KNIGHT'S CASTLE
- ☐ MAGIC BY THE LAKE
- ☐ MAGIC OR NOT?
- ☐ SEVEN-DAY MAGIC
- ☐ THE TIME GARDEN
- ☐ THE WELL-WISHERS

Anne Holm
- ☐ NORTH TO FREEDOM

John R. Tunis
- ☐ IRON DUKE
- ☐ THE DUKE DECIDES
- ☐ CHAMPION'S CHOICE
- ☐ THE KID FROM TOMKINSVILLE
- ☐ WORLD SERIES
- ☐ KEYSTONE KIDS
- ☐ ROOKIE OF THE YEAR
- ☐ ALL-AMERICAN
- ☐ YEA! WILDCATS!
- ☐ A CITY FOR LINCOLN

Henry Winterfeld
- ☐ DETECTIVES IN TOGAS
- ☐ MYSTERY OF THE ROMAN RANSOM

Look for these titles and others in the Odyssey series in your local bookstore.

Or send payment in the form of a check or money order to: HBJ (Operator J), 465 S. Lincoln Drive, Troy, Missouri 63379.

Or call: 1-800-543-1918 (ask for Operator J).

☐ I've enclosed my check payable to Harcourt Brace Jovanovich.

Charge my: ☐ Visa ☐ MasterCard ☐ American Express.

Card Expiration Date

Card #

_____

Signature

_____

Name

_____

Address

_____

City   State   Zip

Please send me _____ copy/copies @ $3.95 each.

($3.95 x no. of copies) $ _____

Subtotal $ _____

Your state sales tax   + $ _____

Shipping and handling (\$1.50 x no. of copies)   + $ _____

Total $ _____

PRICES SUBJECT TO CHANGE